DRAGON'S GAMBIT

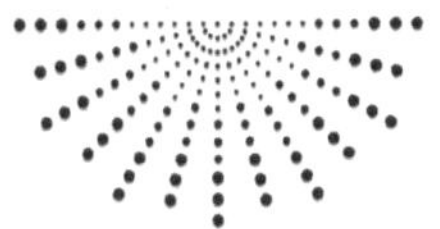

TIEGAN CLYNE

CHAPTER ONE

SEBASTIAN

Soldiers from the Kingdom marched Christopher to their waiting transport while others escorted Patrice more kindly. Their leader, Prince Azanel, sent all of the others away from the farmhouse, the one that supposedly nobody could find. He turned to Sebastian once they were alone.

"My Mate," the prince said, his pale gaze filled with concern. "What did they do to you?"

Sebastian didn't know who this person was, but he knew his face. He had been dreaming of him since he first awoke in the basement of Crown Holdings, an amnesiac prisoner hooked up to a milking machine and used like livestock.

"You don't want to know." He looked around the room. The scent of sex was still hanging in the air. "May I dress?"

Azanel's nostrils flared delicately. "Please shower, too. We have the time."

He went into the attached bathroom and closed the door. He was afraid for Christopher, the captor who was now the captive. The invaders knew that he was related to the ruler of Numea. The things that they might do to his Master, to the man he loved… he didn't want to consider it. He turned on the shower and stepped under the water, washing away the evidence of the night before, wondering if that was the last time he would ever feel Christopher's touch.

He felt bereft.

Sebastian had just begun to feel like he knew his place in this world. His memories, removed by his captors' neural editing, were still as remote as ever, but he had started to feel that he had a way forward, a life that he could understand. Now it had all come crashing down again, leaving him mystified once more.

The door to the bathroom opened, and the uniformed prince came in. Azanel stood watching Sebastian, staring at him through the transparent plastic of the shower door. The look on his face was a mixture of relief and wonder, and it warmed and terrified Sebastian at the same time.

Azanel had called Sebastian his Mate. Could such a thing be possible? What else could explain the prince's presence in his subconscious, a lover who until now had seemingly existed only in his dreamscape? Now he was here, in the flesh, and when Sebastian looked into his undeniably beautiful face, he felt…

Nothing.

The absence of feeling was somehow worse than any rush of emotions could have been. He sensed that Azanel wanted some show of affection, or even a show of distress. He wanted Sebastian to react strongly. That was something he couldn't do, and he didn't know why. If this man was his Mate, shouldn't he have been relieved to see him? And shouldn't he have been furious with Christopher, hating him for all he'd done, instead of worrying about him?

More questions. More confusion. He hated this.

He finished his shower and toweled off. For good or ill, he had grown accustomed to standing naked in the view of strangers, but the way this Azanel looked at him made him embarrassed. He quickly found clean clothes and dressed.

"You lost a scale. I can see the new one growing in," Azanel said, his voice sad and disapproving. Sebastian thought he sounded like someone who had just noticed a scratch on a priceless antique, and the tone didn't help him feel less like a thing.

"It..." He started to say that it was nothing, and in truth, the loss of a scale was the absolute least of the physical damage he had sustained while in the Countess's custody. He wondered whose custody he would be in, now. Somehow he doubted that this supposed prince intended to just set him free... just like he had no idea what he would do with any freedom that might come.

Azanel abruptly strode across the room and took Sebastian in his arms, crushing him to his chest. The dragonel froze, not certain how to react, and after a heartbeat, Azanel released him. They parted awkwardly, and the prince looked away.

"You don't remember me," he said, his voice hollow.

"They did something to my mind," Sebastian told him. "They erased all of my memories. I'm sorry."

It was clear that the news hurt Azanel, but there was also an undertone of annoyance that seemed out of place. The prince said brusquely, "Well, no matter. You will remember me in time. Now we need to take you home."

He took Sebastian's elbow in his hand and started to guide him out of the house. The dragonel pulled away.

"I can walk."

"I just... Of course. My apologies."

In the driveway outside the house, the armored troop transport was idling, waiting for them. Azanel climbed in through the side door, and Sebastian followed, entering the main crew cabin. A group of men in uniform looked up at him. One smiled, but most looked suspicious. Patrice sat between two of the soldiers, one of whom had his weapon pointed at Christopher, who was lying naked on the floor, hogtied and gagged.

"Is that necessary?" Sebastian asked. "He won't..."

"He's a demon," Azanel said flatly. "It's as necessary as it gets."

The soldier to Patrice's left began studying her collar. "We need to get this thing off before it blows us all to fuck."

"I think that's only in response to a remote command," another soldier said. "The only one who could send that order is right here, in no position to do anything."

He illustrated his point by kicking Christopher in the head. Sebastian lunged out of his seat and grabbed the man's ankle in a punishing grip. The soldier cried out.

The dragonel growled, "Do that again, and I'll break your fucking foot off."

"Sebastian!" Azanel shouted, appalled. "What are you doing?"

"He's a prisoner."

"Yes. And your tormentor."

Sebastian looked down into Christopher's eyes, and the brunet shook his head quickly, once. In the dragonel's mind, he said, --*No.*--

The incubus didn't elaborate, but he didn't need to. Sebastian released his hold on the soldier's ankle, vocalizing the only excuse for his actions that he could think of. "You can't abuse prisoners, no matter what they've done. If you do, you're no better than they are."

Azanel's expression softened into something more like pride. "Exactly so. The commander is correct." He looked at the soldier sternly. "No more of that."

Commander?

The soldier looked at Sebastian, then away. "Yes, sir."

Azanel and Sebastian strapped themselves in while the side door closed automatically. The soldier fiddling with Patrice's collar released it with an inhuman growl of disgust.

"I can't get the damned thing off."

"There are buttons or something," Patrice said, trying to help. She gestured toward the captive on the floor of the cabin. "That asshole can probably open it."

Azanel frowned and asked Sebastian, "Is there a chance it will detonate on its own?"

"I don't know," he answered honestly. "There was a remote, but I don't know what happened to it. Let Christopher take it off the way he took off mine."

The soldiers looked at him in suspicion, and he looked back pugnaciously. Azanel unstrapped himself and knelt beside the prisoner.

"I will release your hands and you will remove the collar from Patrice. If you try to escape or try to use your powers in any way, I will kill you. Do you understand?"

Christopher nodded. Azanel took the cuffs from his wrists and stepped back.

The incubus sat up and took the gag out of his mouth. "She needs medical attention," he said. "I was able to do some triage, but she needs more help than I could give here."

Patrice narrowed her eyes. "I'm fine," she said flatly.

"No, you're not. You could have a perforated uterus and if you don't receive proper medical attention, you'll become septic," he disagreed. He rolled up onto his knees, and all the soldiers pointed their rifles at his face. Christopher held up his hands. Without his gloves, the scars from Lord Ashmar's branding irons were plain to see, silhouettes of eagles forever emblazoned on his palms. "Please. Take her to a medical center or a doctor. Don't let her suffer."

"Don't tell us what to do, monster," Azanel growled.

Christopher gestured with his raised and open hands. "If you let me, I'll take her collar off now. Can I approach?"

The prince looked at Patrice. Her face was pale, and anyone could see that she was battling bravely against pain. He nodded. "Carefully. Remember my warning."

"How could I forget?"

He reached up and fingered the controls on the collar, which fell away and landed in her lap. As soon as the felid was freed, Azanel seized Christopher and bound his hands behind his back again. One of the soldiers prepared to gag him, but Sebastian spoke up.

"That's not necessary. He can't do anything to anyone with his voice."

"He can still talk, and I don't want to hear him," the soldier complained.

"You don't understand the power that this beast can wield," the prince told Sebastian. "His voice is one of his weapons."

"He isn't a beast."

That suspicious, judgmental look crawled across most of the men's faces, and Patrice glared at him in disgust.

"Pet," she spat. "Lap dog."

"Quiet." Azanel took the gag and roughly pushed it back into Christopher's mouth, strapping it tightly into place. He shoved their captive back onto the floor and held him there with his foot while he called to the driver. "Let's go."

THE TRANSPORT TOOK them deep into the Badlands. There were no windows in the crew compartment, but from where he sat, Sebastian could see through the driver's windscreen. The terrain they drove through was rocky and barren, a vast expanse of red rocks and silver-gray sand that sparkled like new snow. He saw no life - no animals, no birds, not even any bugs to commit suicide by splattering themselves into the vehicle. Nothing moved but their vehicle, and it seemed like the most godforsaken place he had ever seen.

It took hours of riding in stony silence, but they finally reached a heavily-guarded military base surrounded by electrified fencing. The perimeter bristled with artillery. As they waited at the checkpoint, a set of fighter jets screamed through the sky, leaving the base, emblazoned with the image of a dragon's head. It was the same electronic sound that had shattered his sleep that morning, and it set his teeth on edge.

They were waved through the gate and entered the compound. They drove past buildings and soldiers and piles of the material of war. The bustling of the soldiers and the squat buildings felt familiar, and Sebastian strained to remember when or whether he'd been in this place before. His mind remained blank, and he clenched his teeth in frustration.

Beside him, Azanel watched him closely. Sebastian looked back at him, wondering what the ice dragon was thinking. He felt like he should have known, or should have been able to predict, how Azanel would act or react, especially since he was supposedly Sebastian's Mate. He felt and understood nothing.

The vehicle rolled to a stop outside what was clearly the command center, and the soldiers scrambled out as a unit, taking Christopher and Patrice with them. Sebastian started to follow, but Azanel put a hand on his arm.

"This way," he said.

He reached out with his mind, hoping that his lover would hear him. *--Christopher...--*

-- Don't worry about me. I'll be fine. Just be careful.-- A rush

of warmth came to him through their telepathy. *--I love you. Don't forget that.--*

--How could I?-- He swallowed his fear. *--I love you, too.--*

Christopher shut off the communication, and Sebastian knew that whatever happened from here on, he was on his own.

Azanel led Sebastian into the command center. Banks of computers and telemetry equipment hummed in neat rows, each one manned by a serious-faced soldier. An officer in dark fatigues looked up when they came in, and he smiled broadly, revealing pointed teeth.

"Mission accomplished, Prince Azanel. Well done."

"The Flying Dragons will always come through." He looked at Sebastian with a smile. "We said we would rescue Commander Goxtli, and we have."

"So I see." There was tension in the officer's voice, and it made Sebastian wary. He sensed that he was hardly this officer's favorite person. "Welcome back, Commander. You were gone for a very long time."

He had no idea what to say, so he only said, "Yes, sir."

Azanel said, "Commander Goxtli, this is General Doz."

"He knows me."

"Not anymore," the ice dragon said. "They did something to eliminate his memories."

General Doz looked at Sebastian with narrowed eyes. "Interesting."

"That's not the word I would choose," the dragonel responded dryly. "I don't remember any of you, but this base looks familiar, so I'm taking that as a positive sign. How long was I gone?"

Azanel answered. "Nearly a year."

The dragonel's jaw dropped open. "A year? But..."

His voice trailed off. He could only really remember a month's time, perhaps a little more, between his awakening in the basement of Crown Holdings and the moment he found himself in now. He had known that he was missing time, but the sheer volume of that deficit stunned him. His palms grew slick.

The general walked away briefly, pacing with his shoulders rigid. The back of his uniform was split to allow a ridge of dorsal plates to protrude through the slit in the fabric. A long, thick tail grew from the base of his spine, similarly freed from the confines of the uniform, and it swayed as he walked, the barbed tip flicking. Sebsatian had no idea what manner of creature the general was.

General Doz turned back around and faced them. "Prince Azanel, please escort him to sickbay. He'll need to be evaluated for injuries and other conditions."

"And then?" Sebastian asked.

"And then you'll be sent for debriefing."

There was a strange tone in the general's voice. Sebastian asked, "Debriefing, or deprogramming?"

General Doz smiled tightly. "That all depends on what they find in medical."

Azanel put a hand on Sebastian's shoulder. "Let's go."

"Make sure the docs send me a full report."

"Yes, sir."

They left the command center. A pair of young officers looked at Sebastian as they passed, recognition in their expressions, but Sebastian had no idea who they were or how they knew him. They looked happy to see him, though, wide smiles breaking across their faces. He nodded to them, and Azanel leaned closer to him.

"Everyone is thrilled to have you back." He whispered, "Don't worry. If the enemy comes, I won't let them take you again."

Sebastian looked over at the dragon as they walked. He echoed, "Again?"

Azanel's pale face flushed and he looked away. "When Pentepolis took you, I... I failed to protect you. It was my fault that you were taken."

He stopped. "How was it your fault?"

Azanel wouldn't meet his gaze, a reticence that put Sebsatian on his guard. "I was with you when they came. We were at my lake house, and I'd made the mistake of sending the guard detail away."

The words made his brain tingle unpleasantly, something that mystified him. A headache blossomed behind his eyes. "Guard detail?"

"Your bodyguards."

"I had bodyguards?" Sebastian frowned, confused. "Why?"

Azanel finally looked at him again, and he smiled. "Because you're the heir to the Golden Throne, of course." The words seemed to be in keeping with what he'd already been told, but the concept was alien. Azanel faced him and put his hands on Sebastian's shoulders. "This is just one of the many things that I will remind you of," he said. He leaned in and kissed Sebastian gently, barely more than a whisper against his lips. "And I will remind you of it all if you'll let me."

Sebastian did not return the kiss, and he could feel how his lack of a welcoming response caused Azanel deep disappointment. The dragon stepped back and looked away, both hurt and annoyed.

"Well," he said, his voice tight. "Let's get you to the doctors."

～

CHRISTOPHER

THE GUARDS DRAGGED Christopher and Patrice in separate directions, taking her toward a large building and dragging him toward what was clearly a stockade. Their grips were like iron, and they led him over the roughest possible parts of the terrain, a special consideration for his bare feet. He had no doubt that the cuts and bruises he was receiving were only the beginning of the unpleasantries that he was about to experience. The men who now held him captive were no friends of his, and he knew that their hatred of him and the rest of Pentepolis would soon be unleashed.

He could hardly blame them.

Every military base he'd ever been in smelled the same, and this one was no exception. Motor oil, gunpowder, sweat and the pervasive dusty smell of the Badlands triggered memories he'd rather have forgotten. He remembered the camp he'd been brought to when he'd first reached this world, as well as the things Lord Ashmar and his men had done to him. His palms ached, and he clenched his fists. He had been through unpleasantries before, and suffered through pain applied by masters of the art. These soldiers were amateurs in that respect. He could endure this.

They reached the stockade, a squat concrete building constructed entirely out of cinder blocks and poured concrete. The front door lock opened with an electronic key that one of the men carried, and Christopher made note of which pocket that key was returned to. Once the door was open, he was shoved into a concrete-floored hallway with cells on both sides, their walls and doors entirely made of steel bars. The guards dragged him to a cell at the back of the building, one with steel plates for walls, and they threw him in. Christopher landed on his side, but he rolled to his feet as quickly as he could, no mean feat considering he was still handcuffed with his hands behind his back. Three of the four guards came into the cell with him while the fourth stood guard outside the closed steel plate door.

One of the guards, a reptilian creature with an elongated snout and greenish-gray scaly skin, stepped forward with his hands balled into fists. "You like kidnapping people and using them as sex slaves, huh?"

Christopher stood and faced him, trying his best to look defiant despite the gag that was making him drool. The guard grabbed his face.

"Shoe's on the other foot now, you son of a bitch."

He punched Christopher in the stomach. The incubus doubled over in pain, the air pushed out of his lungs in a rush. The guard grabbed him by the head and flung him to the concrete floor, where he landed painfully on his face. The man knelt over him, straddling Christopher's body, and he heard a zipper.

It didn't take a genius to know what was coming next.

"See how you like it," the guard about to rape him hissed. He punctuated his words with an appropriately reptilian hiss, and Christopher wondered what manner of creature he was. He seemed to be part alligator, and he wished that he could examine him. A quick telepathic touch told him that the other two were lupen, native wolf shifters, but this one... he was a mystery.

The guard's cock breached him abruptly with no preamble, and Christopher grunted at the sudden pain. One of the other men laughed.

"Yes! Get it, Creek!"

Creek thrust violently into Christopher's hole, each hard stroke jolting the incubus's entire body. His own erection sprang to life immediately, and he groaned, letting the pain and pleasure mingle. Heat ran up his spine from his asshole to his back, and he lifted his hips to thrust back at the other man, encouraging Creek to keep going. Creek seized his hips in a punishing grip, holding him still.

"Fuck," one of the lupen guards said. "The sick little bastard likes it."

Christopher closed his eyes and reached out with his demonic powers. The delicious red energy of Creek's anger and violent passion filled him, and Christopher sucked it in. His weeping dick head rubbed against the concrete floor, and the painful stimulation added to the sensation of being roughly fucked. He moaned in delight, tightening around Creek's rod.

Creek gasped and came, and the energy he released flooded into Christopher, who drank it down like fine wine. He felt it burning in his solar plexus, strengthening the little hellfire that already blazed within him.

One of the other guards took Creek's place, and the remaining man grabbed Christopher's hair and yanked his head up. Creek took the gag out of the incubus's mouth, and the third guard replaced it with hot, hard flesh. Christopher sucked him eagerly, his tongue and throat working the man's cock.

"Shit!" the guard exclaimed, face-fucking him until Christopher's neck ached from it. He gagged against the intrusion, and the violence made him shiver with abandon. More red energy coiled around him, released haphazardly by these men who thought that they were hurting him, and he pulled it in. He opened his hands, pressing his palms against the belly of the man who was railing him, but he hesitated just shy of stealing the guard's soul. There would be time for that sort of thing later.

"Fucker! Move those hands!"

Creek kicked Christopher in the side, something that did little to distract him from the two cocks that filled his holes. The pain from the blow added to his pleasure, and the incubus moaned again. The guard behind him shuddered into orgasm, filling Christopher's body with his cum and with his energy. He pulled free, muttering and shoving his soiled cock back into his uniform. The third guard climaxed deep inside the incubus' throat, and Christopher swallowed his hot offering, taking energy and semen into himself.

"Fuck," Creek grumbled. "Sick asshole."

Christopher rolled onto his side, grinning. "Does your other buddy want a turn? 'Cause I'm not quite done."

Creek stepped forward and kicked him in the stomach. Christopher absorbed the blow and curled into a protective ball as much as he could with his hands behind his back. The angry guard pulled back his foot for another kick, and one of his fellows stopped him.

"Don't," he warned. "It's one thing to have a little fun with him, but the General wants him for questioning, and you know we can't kill him."

Creek relented. Christopher looked up at him, and the man's face was twisted in an angry snarl that revealed long canines and a startlingly red tongue. He spat in Christopher's face.

"It's your lucky day, fucker," Creek growled. He stalked out of the cell, taking his companions with him. The door slammed shut, and the fourth guard, the one who hadn't touched him, looked through the barred window at Christopher, who looked back and shifted into a reasonably comfortable position, sitting on the floor. The guard's eyes flickered down to the incubus's erection, still unsatisfied and bobbing in the air.

*--Come on in and play,-- *Christopher invited. *--I won't tell.--*

The guard recoiled and turned away. His mind was thoroughly human, which made him easier to manipulate than the others. That was helpful information that Christopher filed away for later use.

It was strange, he thought, that they left the easiest mark to guard him. He smelled a trap. He had learned a long time ago that if a door was left more or less open, it was because he was intended to go through it. He could take advantage of the human's weak will, or he could wait and take the temperature of the situation.

He would bide his time, for now.

--*Sebastian,*-- he called out, not certain his dragonel would hear him, and even less certain he would want to. --*Don't resist them. Don't give them an excuse to hurt you.*--

He hoped that somewhere, somehow, Sebastian had heard.

CHAPTER TWO

SEBASTIAN

*I*n the corridor leading to the medical center, Christopher's voice whispered in Sebastian's mind, and he sighed with relief at the sound. If his Master was speaking to him this way, from such a distance, it meant that he was healthy and awake. He was determined to obey for now.

--Christopher,-- he thought back, hoping his keeper would hear. *--I will find you.--*

His chuckle responded with gratifying speed. *--Not if I find you first.--*

Azanel put his hand on Sebastian's elbow and guided him around a blind corner, something that made the dragonel tense for an attack that never came. Instead, he found himself faced with a double door that Azanel walked through. Sebastian followed.

On the other side was a medical center, and though the dragonel knew next to nothing about such things, it looked to be modern and well-equipped. To his relief, there were no milking machines anywhere in evidence. He hoped those days were gone.

A white-haired human wearing wire-rimmed glasses turned and looked at them with a broad smile. He came forward. "Commander Goxtli! How wonderful to see you looking so well! We were thrilled with the news that you'd been rescued at last." He turned his smile onto Azanel. "Well done, Your Highness. My compliments to the Flying Dragons."

Azanel nodded his blond head. "It was our honor."

Sebastian spoke to the doctor. "General Doz has sent me here for an examination."

"I'm not surprised. You were captive for a very long time, and the Five Cities and especially the Community aren't known for their kindness." The doctor gestured toward an exam room. "After you, sir."

Azanel began to follow them, but the doctor stopped him at the door.

"Your Highness, I must ask you to please wait outside."

His eyes narrowed and he considered the doctor angrily. He clearly didn't like being separated from Sebastian, which should have made the dragonel feel protected. It just made him feel like a toy to be owned.

"Fine," Azanel said at last. "But I'll be right outside."

"Of course."

The doctor held the door for Sebastian, and the dragonel walked in. As soon as they were inside, the doctor closed the door and flipped a switch, and thick panels made of acoustic tiles descended from the ceiling, covering all four walls and obscuring the doors and windows. A fine mist filled the room, bringing with it the smell of chemicals.

"Sound deadening," the doctor explained. "Nobody outside will hear anything that's done or said in here."

Sebastian backed away from the man and scanned the room. There was an examination table, a counter with many drawers, and nothing else. No milking machine, no chains, no open threats. He still kept his back to the wall and watched warily as the doctor came further into the room. The man crossed his arms and leaned against the counter.

"I understand your distrust, and I don't blame you, but I assure you that I am no threat to you. I'm here to help."

Sebastian withheld judgment and stayed silent.

The man sighed. "My name is Willard Montez, and I've been a doctor with the Kingdom's army for twenty years. You and I were once acquainted, believe it or not, before your capture."

"I don't remember you."

"I know. Neural disruption is the first thing they do with any prisoner, and it would have been in their best interests to remove all memory of who you are and what you've been trained to do." Dr. Montez smiled. "You'd be far too dangerous to them if you were in full command of yourself."

It was strange for Sebastian to imagine himself as dangerous, but in retrospect, they had always treated him as some kind of threat. All the armed guards, the manacles, the imprisonment... it made sense now, in a way. It had never occurred to him that his captors had been just as afraid of him as he had been of them.

He wondered now what it was about him that they feared.

Dr. Montez made no effort to approach him. "Do you want to tell me what they did to you? Perhaps point me toward the injuries you have?"

"I..." He shook his head. "No."

"You must have a lot of questions for me."

He had nothing but questions, but he didn't trust this man enough to ask them. "I don't."

Montez raised an eyebrow. "Well. That's interesting." He picked up a clipboard and made a note on the paper that it held. "Tell me… what are your feelings toward the Countess?"

Sebastian watched the doctor warily. "I'm not a fan."

"No? Why?"

He fixed a hard look onto the human's face. "You must be joking. You know what she does, what she's responsible for."

"Do I?" He smiled, and Sebastian rankled at the almost smug expression. "Why don't you tell me?"

He took a breath and walked a little further from Montez, heading toward the back of the room where he could stand in the corner and protect himself if need be. At least there would be two approaches that enemies couldn't use if they intended to come for him.

"I'd rather not."

"Why? Because it's sexual?"

His question showed that he *did* know what the Countess did, and Sebastian narrowed his eyes at the disingenuous tone. This was a psych test.

"Because it's embarrassing."

"You must feel a great deal of shame about the way that you were treated."

The dragonel raised his chin and stood tall. "What I feel is not your concern."

"Isn't it? If you're in pain, I'm here to help you." Montez smiled kindly. Sebastian distrusted that look. It concealed a multitude of lies. "If your loyalties are confused, I'm here to give you clarity."

Ah. There it is.

"My loyalties are secure."

"And who are you loyal to?" The question was asked in a mild but searching tone. "The Kingdom? The King?" He looked into Sebastian's eyes. "Christopher?"

He tried not to react, but he could feel his expression flicker. He clenched his teeth and cursed himself for revealing anything, and he only hoped that the doctor misinterpreted what he'd seen, whatever that had been. Sebastian's emotions were conflicted where his former captor was concerned. He loved him, yes, or thought he did, but Christopher had also misused him and controlled him in ways he found hard to forgive. He wasn't certain if anything he thought or felt was genuine and not imposed upon him by the incubus and his ilk. It was maddening.

"I'm loyal to myself."

The human nodded and adjusted a control on the wall.

Sebastian tried to wrap his head around it. Crown Holdings and his experiences there seemed unreal to him now, and his memories were beginning to jumble together and make him confused. The milking machine. The Countess's dinner party. Christopher's hands, gentle and loving. The orderly named Michael. The basement room. The apartment at the Countess's estate. Images and sensations flashed through him, disjointed and disorienting.

The smell of the mist was stronger and becoming unpleasant. Dr. Montez continued to smile at him, but Sebastian's vision was beginning to swim. His fingers tingled, and he looked down at them. Claws were growing where his fingernails had been, and the golden scales dusted across his skin began to expand, growing larger and more dense. His chest felt tight and full, as if he had been holding his breath, and he exhaled heavily. To his startled amazement, a jet of bluish flame escaped his lips and burned the mist away, the fire extending from him by nearly a foot.

He looked up at Dr. Montez in fear, expecting to be punished, but the doctor only smiled and nodded.

"Good," he said. "You're coming back to yourself."

"What am I?"

"A dragonel. You are the natural-born son of King Goxtli,

the Keeper of the Golden Throne and king of the gold drag-ons, and his ifrit bride Alamna. Their only child."

Sebastian's head whirled. "Natural-born. Not lab-created."

Dr. Montez straightened. The chemical was filling the room, now, clinging to the floor and rising around their legs in clouds that reached as high as mid-thigh. The doctor pulled a gas mask out of one of the drawers and put it on.

Sebastian's body shook, and his legs felt like jelly. He tried to put his hand out to steady himself against the wall, but his arm would not obey. He stumbled toward the door and fell against the examination table, his claws digging into the plastic covering the padded surface. He turned an accusing glare onto the human doctor.

"What are you doing to me?"

"Don't fight it," the doctor advised. "This will all be over soon."

His body was useless. He groaned and clenched his teeth, and his jaws felt different than before, elongating slowly. His teeth were pointed now, and felt alien to himself.

Sebastian glared at the doctor and growled. His own voice was unfamiliar. "God damn you," he managed to spit between grinding teeth.

The doctor smiled down at him as he tumbled to the floor. "I'm sure he will."

AZANEL

DR. MONTEZ EMERGED from the examination room, wiping his hands with a paper towel, and Azanel stood from the chair where he'd been waiting for the last hour. The doctor smiled and nodded to the dragon prince.

"He's been brutalized, as we expected, but he's in good health otherwise. The gas overcame the suppressants that they filled him with, and he was able to take his alternate form. I removed an RFID chip from the back of his neck, and it's been sent to the lab for investigation." He tossed the towel aside. "He's going to be furious when he wakes up, but you'll be able to explain our reasons for tranquilizing him."

"Will you release him to me?"

"Of course. He'll be waking up in a few minutes. Once he's awake, go ahead and take him to the debriefing." He held up his clipboard. "I've just got to finish making some notes."

Azanel shook the doctor's hand, then entered the room. Sebastian was lying naked on his side on the examination table, an oxygen mask over his face. He had resumed his human form, and Azanel was disappointed. He had hoped to see his Alter. There were few dragonels as beautiful as Sebastian when they assumed their full draconic splendor.

He left the room again, activating the noise cancelling on the way out. He glanced around and made sure he was alone. From a pocket in his uniform, he pulled out a cell phone and placed a call to the only programmed number. Azanel waited for the person on the other side to pick up.

A woman's voice answered with gratifying speed. "Well? Have we had a happy reunion?"

"He doesn't have any memory of me," he complained.

"Was that a requirement?"

The sound of her smug voice annoyed him, and anger flashed through him, making his back tingle where his dorsal spines would be in his other form. "That was supposed to be arranged."

"We implanted the images you requested," she defended, untroubled. "His mind is complex and it was difficult to manipulate properly. He might not have conscious memories, but I assure you, you're in his subconscious."

"That wasn't the outcome we agreed upon."

She laughed. "We agreed to make the attempt. We never guaranteed any outcomes."

"If he doesn't acknowledge me as his Mate..."

"That part is up to you. We wiped his mind and planted specific memories per your request. As for your little romantic fairy tale? Seduce him. Win him. His emotions were never my concern."

Azanel grumbled, "We're not done talking about this."

"Oh, I think we are." Her voice went cold. "You have what you paid for. Now it's up to you to make the best of it."

She hung up on him, narrowly beating him to the punch. Azanel tucked the phone back into his pocket and returned to the examination room. When he opened the door, the dragonel stirred, and Azanel put his hand on Sebastian's shoulder. Sebastian blinked his golden eyes and looked up at Azanel with a total lack of recognition. The emptiness in that look made him angry. This was not how things were supposed to be happening.

He concealed his annoyance and smiled gently. "How are you feeling?"

The dragonel reached up and pulled the oxygen mask away. He flung it across the room. "Sick of this shit."

Azanel raised his eyebrows. He had never known Sebastian to be profane. "I'm sorry. They wanted to be able to examine you without hurting you, and without you hurting them."

He sat up shakily and turned to hang his feet over the side of the table. "I can handle pain. I don't appreciate the knockout gas."

"He was trying to be considerate."

Sebastian glowered. "If everyone would just stop doing

me favors, that would be great."

Azanel took Sebastian's hand, and the dragonel looked down at their shared grip. He pulled his hand away. Azanel burned.

"I need to take you back to General Doz," he told him. "For your debriefing."

Sebastian laughed, and it was a cynical sound. He looked around. "Where are my clothes?"

He indicated the neat pile on the floor. "Right there."

The dragonel shakily set about getting dressed, clearly still feeling the effects of the gas. Azanel tried to help steady him, but Sebastian stepped away from his touch. Stung by the repeated rejection, Azanel let him go.

When he was dressed, Sebastian turned to face him. "Let's get this over with."

CHRISTOPHER

CHRISTOPHER'S CELL door opened and he stood up to face his visitor. A reptilian humanoid in a military uniform strode in, his pointed teeth revealed in an unfriendly grin.

"Well, well. What have we here? Countess Balika's grandson." He walked closer and stood in front of Christopher, his arms crossed over his broad chest. "What do you suppose she'll give to get you back?"

He snorted. "A whole lot of nothing. There's not a lot of familial warmth there, in case you're interested."

"I know what it means among demons when you call someone your grandmother, and I know she's no blood of yours." He nodded. "She owns your soul."

"My marker," he corrected. "My soul is still my own."

"Bullshit. Marker and soul, they're the same thing."

Christopher smiled. "Not exactly, but I wouldn't expect a… what are you, exactly? A troglodyte?"

"I'm the general in charge of this base, and your life is in my hands," he growled. "You're going to tell me everything you know about the Numean forces, and about that bitch who owns you."

He looked the creature in the eye. "No. I'm not."

"You think you're going to win this? Do you really think your will is strong enough to keep us from finding out what we want to know?" the general scoffed.

Christopher squared his shoulders. "There's only one way to find out."

The general walked to the cell door and called through the bars. "Junko. Now."

The guard opened the door, and another uniformed creature, this one with feathers instead of hair and three-fingered hands, came into the room. He was pushing a cart that had been covered with a surgical drape.

The troglodyte officer smiled broadly. "I'll just leave you two to become better acquainted."

Christopher eyed the feathered humanoid as he approached. The creature clacked his beak and laughed.

"Oppressor," he trilled, his voice warbly. "This will be my pleasure."

"Mine, too," he said, smiling seductively. He licked his lip.

"No. It won't." The birdman, Junko, turned. "Guards, come in."

Creek and the human who had been standing outside the door came in, and their eyes were hard. Christopher backed up warily. The two guards seized him and threw him onto the floor, where they pinned him on his back with his hands trapped beneath him.

"Good, good," the birdman beamed. His smile made his beak seem even wider than before, and it made his face grotesque. "Hold him. Prevent him from touching you. His palms can do damage."

"What kind of damage?" Creek asked, sounding startled.

"Take your spirit," Junko said. "Eat it up."

They were right, after a fashion, but wrong as well. He could still take the spirit, but he'd never be able to consume it. Thanks to the alchemy of the brands in his palms, any souls he took would be funneled directly to Lord Ashmar, and he would be damned if he strengthened that bastard one iota.

The guards held him still and the birdman leaned over him with a hypodermic filled with a silvery liquid. He injected it into the side of Christopher's neck, directly into the vein, and within seconds his head felt like it was exploding. He groaned against the pain. Junko watched his face carefully, gauging his reactions. Christopher tried to keep his face impassive, but the burning in his head was like nothing he had ever felt. This was not the sort of pain he could enjoy.

"Almost there," Junko chirred, sounding well pleased with himself.

Creek asked, "What is that?"

"It short-circuits the pleasure center in the brain," the birdman answered proudly. "Even though this monster is a known masochist, he will feel no pleasure from what we are about to do."

"How do you know he's a masochist?" Creek asked.

"The walls have eyes." Junko glared at him. "And you should be ashamed of yourself."

The burning inside Christopher's skull was beginning to taper off, and he found himself gasping for breath, reeling from the strange sensation. Junko nodded.

"Good. Let's begin."

CHAPTER THREE

SEBASTIAN

*A*zanel led Sebastian through the halls of the command center until they reached a featureless room furnished only with a low, makeshift table and a single chair before it.

"Sit down," Azanel commanded, and Sebastian obeyed. The ice dragon smiled thinly. "I'll go and see if General Doz is ready. Do you want something to drink?"

Sebastian nodded. His throat was dry from the gas he'd inhaled. "Water would be nice."

"Of course."

Azanel left, and for the first time since his rude awakening that morning, Sebastian was on his own. He ran a hand over his face, still feeling the effects of the sedation. He was furious with Dr. Montez, yes, but mostly he was tired. Tired of being messed with, tired of being the only one who had no idea what was going on. He resented the technology, whatever it had been, that had removed his memories, and he wondered if the process could even be reversed. The only one he could think of who might have that answer was Christopher, and he had no idea where his... lover? Master?

Owner? He struggled to even come up with the right word to use. Sebastian only knew that Christopher was out there, a captive, and he was worried about him.

The door to the room opened, and a soldier came in. His uniform was the same green as the tactical outfits worn by the unit who had raided Christopher's farmhouse, and his face was familiar. He was the one who had smiled at Sebastian when he'd first boarded the troop carrier.

The man came to stand in front of the table where the dragonel was sitting, and he smiled down at him hesitantly. "Hi," he said.

Sebastian frowned. "Hello."

The man - a completely normal, human man, as far as he could tell - licked his lips nervously. "It's, uh… it's good to see you again. It's been a long time."

He racked his brain, trying to find some spark of recognition, but nothing kindled. He sighed. "I'm sorry… I don't think I know you."

The man's face fell, and his blue eyes clouded with troubled emotions before he looked away. "Yeah, about that… I heard that the Numeans used their neural editing procedure on you. Tough break."

Sebastian watched the man's hands. He was picking at the tabletop, his fingernails catching on the grain of the unfinished wood. It was a nervous gesture, one that concealed emotional turmoil.

He looked up at the human. "It hurts you that I don't remember."

"I… well, yeah. We've known each other for a long time. Went to basic together and…" He looked up, finally meeting Sebastian's gaze once more. "My name is Lieutenant Cavan Waters. We served together in the King's Talons."

He had no memory of this man, but he felt that he should have. The name of the unit stirred something in him, a bellicose and proud part that had been dormant until that moment, and it surprised him to find something so martial within himself. He swallowed.

"I'm Sebastian."

Cavan grinned. "I know. I'm not the one with the memory problem, and I would never forget you."

His words carried a heavy weight of emotion, and Sebastian rose to his feet. "Were we... close?"

Cavan swallowed. "Brothers in arms. Served together for almost fifteen years, if you include academy time. Yeah. We were close."

The dragonel closed his eyes briefly. "I'm sorry."

"Don't be," the man said, forcing a smile. "I'm sure you'll remember everything in time. Those mind wipes can't be that good, can they?"

He huffed a semi-laugh. "They're good enough."

Cavan's eyes met his, and they were the color of deep ocean. How Sebastian knew what a deep ocean looked like was another question. "Don't let them rush you," he counseled. "If you're meant to remember something, you will. What's meant to be will always find a way."

There was something about that saying that seemed familiar, and it brought the beginnings of a crooked smile to Sebastian's face. The door opened, and Cavan straightened immediately, pulling his lanky body to attention. General Doz and Prince Azanel came in, both scowling at the interloper.

"This isn't social hour," Doz barked. "Back to your post, soldier."

"Yes, sir." Cavan saluted and left, his eyes sliding once toward the dragonel as he went. Azanel closed the door with a scowl and Sebastian sat down again.

Doz had a file in his hands, and he flipped through the papers inside. "Doc says you've got a torn-off scale, healing wounds on your buttocks from a whip…"

"It was a cane."

Doz glanced up at Sebastian, then returned to his report. "Torn tissues that were surgically repaired on your asshole…"

"Don't be vulgar," Azanel scolded.

"… and you were hopped up on suppressant drugs to keep you from your true nature. They took care of that with the gas."

"Is that what it was for?" Sebastian commented, annoyed. "He could have asked."

"Your permission was not required."

"How unusual."

His sarcasm brought a raised eyebrow from the general, but Azanel smiled. The ice dragon said, "Well, that sounds more like the old Sebastian."

Doz tossed the file down on the table in front of the dragonel. Vivid photographs of his injuries lay on top of the papers. Sebastian looked at them in distant curiosity, then turned his gaze to the general's unfriendly face.

"That's the physical stuff. Now it's time for you to tell me everything they did."

Azanel leaned against the wall directly across from Sebastian, his arms crossed, his eyes cool. His expression was unreadable.

"I'll tell you what I remember," the dragonel said, "but they removed almost all of my memories, so for the most part I'm at a loss."

"Get talking," Doz commanded.

"General," Azanel interjected, "mind your tone. Remember to whom you're speaking."

Sebastian sat back. "Before I tell you anything, I need to know what happened to the two people who were brought here with me."

"The felid and the Oppressor?"

"Yes. Are they all right?"

Doz's eyes narrowed, and his slit pupils pinched. "Why do you care about the Oppressor?"

"He doesn't need to explain himself," Azanel interjected.

"The hell he doesn't!" Doz planted his palms on the table in front of Sebastian, startling the dragonel and reminding him of his captivity. The general leaned over the dragonel, his lips pulled back from his pointed teeth. "You were there in their hands for a year. That's enough time to turn you against us. And now you're asking about the well-being of the Oppressor, a man whose very existence is a slap in the face to all of us in Mythria. And you think you don't need to explain yourself?"

Sebastian met Doz's glare, and he found the courage to glare back. "I want to know what's happening to him, because I want justice to be served. And as for Patrice, she was a fellow prisoner, and I'm concerned for her safety. Now answer the question, or I'm not telling you shit."

"You are in no position to deny us," the general warned.

"What are you going to do? Torture it out of me?" Sebastian challenged. He could feel heat gathering in his chest, and he wondered if that was where the flames he'd breathed in the doctor's office had come from. If so, the thought of belching fire into Doz's face was appealing.

Azanel tried to placate him. "We aren't your enemies."

"Really? As far as I know, everyone is my enemy." He stood, the chair scraping across the floor. "I've been grabbed out of bed, taken into custody, subjected to knock-out gas, and now you're insisting that I answer questions to your satisfaction when I don't even know who any of you people are. It's just more hoops for me to jump through, and I am tired of jumping. So fuck you."

Doz straightened. "Sit down, Commander."

His first instinct was to obey, but instead he set his jaw. "Make me."

Azanel gaped at him. "Sebastian!"

The general grabbed the file and snarled, "You're going to deprogramming. We're going to get that Numean attitude beaten out of you."

Azanel growled, "You wouldn't dare!"

Both Doz and Sebastian looked at Azanel, surprised by his vehemence. The ice dragon stepped forward, invading Doz's space and glaring down at the shorter male.

"Excuse me?" the general challenged.

Azanel punctuated his words with a finger jab into the officer's chest. "This is no common soldier you're bullying. This is the Crown Prince of Mythria, heir to the Golden Throne, and you will show him respect!"

He pointed at Sebastian. "He is a brainwashed tool of the enemy and I will be damned if I send him back to the King before I know he's not a threat!"

"No deprogramming!" Azanel thundered. "He is no threat! He's wounded. There's a difference!"

The two stood and glared at one another, nearly vibrating in their anger. Sebastian stood up and went to stand beside Azanel, who glanced at him and moved slightly in front of him, his body language protective. Doz's narrowed eyes turned to Sebastian's face, then back to the ice dragon.

"You are responsible," he finally said. "If he does *anything*, if he hurts *anybody*, it's on your royal head."

Azanel nodded, satisfied. "I understand. And I assure you, he won't hurt anyone who doesn't try to hurt him first."

Sebastian told the general, "I will not go quietly for deprogramming. Be warned."

The general glanced down at Sebastian's chest. The scales were backlit by a golden glow that made them stand out like silhouettes, and the light shone through the thin fabric of his

T-shirt. Azanel looked as well, and he put a hand on Sebastian's shoulder.

"Stand down, Your Highness," he advised. His use of the honorific seemed more for the general's benefit than for any sort of propriety or etiquette. It was a reminder of the position that Sebastian supposedly held, even though the dragonel felt no connection to the words. He felt no connection to any of this.

The general considered the situation for a moment, then said, "Tell me what they did to you."

As unemotionally as he could, Sebastian told them the story. "The first thing I remember is waking up in some sort of harness rig, hanging from the ceiling while Lord Ashmar taunted me about getting caught while running away. Then they kept me in their facility for several weeks, and they..." He swallowed and forced out the words. "They milked me for semen so they could create more dragonels. They told me that they'd made me in a lab, but I think that was a lie."

"It *was* a lie," Azanel said, his fair face reddening in anger. "And how dare they! Were there any offspring created?"

"They said that there were eight pregnancies in progress," he answered.

Azanel slammed his hand onto the table in a rage, and the wood snapped beneath the blow. Doz chuckled.

"Temper, temper," he mocked. He turned back to Sebastian. "What else?"

"They paraded me for the Community and subjected me to punishment. I tried to run away again, and Christopher brought me back. Then the raid happened, and Christopher took me, Rupert and Patrice to the farmhouse where you found us." He set his jaw. "You didn't have to kill Rupert."

"He attacked us," Azanel sniffed.

"He'd never attack anybody."

"That *creature* was a disgrace. Killing him was a mercy."

"I want more details," Doz told Sebastian, interrupting the princes' disagreement. "What's your relationship with the Oppressor?"

It made his head hurt, but he lied, "He was my Master."

Azanel looked like he was going to be ill. "Your Master? You have no Master, Sebastian. You are a prince!"

"Programming," Doz said, nodding. "They broke you."

Sebastian nodded. "Maybe."

The general turned to Azanel. "You see? They could have implanted anything in him. Suggestions. Triggers. It's too dangerous to return him to the Golden Hall."

"I don't want to go to the Golden Hall," Sebastian told them. They both turned and looked at him in surprise. "I don't want anything to do with you people. I want to take Christopher and leave."

Azanel looked stung. "You love him," he accused. "Don't you?"

Doz made a disgusted sound and turned away, snatching the file from the floor where it had fallen. Sebastian answered as honestly as he could.

"I don't know. Sometimes I think so, and sometimes I can't stand what he's done, and sometimes I... "

Doz growled in the back of his throat, and it was a feral and animal sound. "I never thought I'd see a gold dragonel succumb to that sort of petty brainwashing." He pointed at Sebastian. "You have been compromised."

Azanel asked, "Where would you take him, if you were allowed to do that?"

"I don't know," he admitted. "Away."

"And do what?"

"I don't know."

"Return him to the Countess?" Doz mocked. "Is that what you'd do?"

Sebastian spoke before he could stop himself. "Christopher hates and fears the Countess. He'd never want to go back there."

The ice dragon shook his head. "But he's her accomplice. He has been for generations. He's been her right-hand torturer…"

"No. That's Lord Ashmar."

Doz opened his mouth to speak, but he was interrupted when the door to the room opened. A woman in a tan uniform with gold buttons came in and handed a computer tablet to the general. She was beautiful, with thick black hair bound up into a neat chignon. Her eyes were hazel, but almost amber in hue, and from the look they held, she was not one to suffer any nonsense.

"His Majesty's demands," she said. Her voice had a strange quality, as if there were multiple people speaking at once, and it made Sebastian's ears ring.

Doz looked at the tablet with a scowl. "Is he kidding?"

The woman's face was stony. "His Majesty doesn't kid."

"Fine." He handed the tablet back. "I'll see that it happens."

She saluted, then turned to Sebastian and bowed. "Your Highness. It's a relief to see you again."

"Thank you," he said, sounding as bewildered as he felt. She studied his face for a moment, then backed up a step before she turned and left the room.

Azanel asked, "Well?"

Doz glared and slapped the tablet against his leg. "Take him to the king."

CHAPTER FOUR

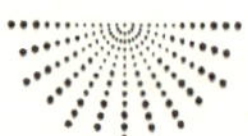

CHRISTOPHER

Christopher curled on his side, shaking, as Junko removed his probes but left the alchemical silver pellets buried deep in each muscle to prolong his misery. Creek and the other guard stood by the door to the cell, unnerved by what they had witnessed. Claw marks in the concrete floor surrounded the incubus, and the cart that had held Junko's equipment was shattered in the corner, flung there by demonic power.

"Well," the birdman said. "We have what we wanted. The general will be pleased."

The human guard shook his head. "That was... I don't have words."

"Effective," Junko said. "It was effective."

The cell door opened, and the two lupen guards came in with a heavy tarp. They put it over Christopher's body and rolled him in it, tying the tarp closed with ropes and wrapping him up like an obscene gift. Junko carried his machine out with him, and Creek, the largest of the four guards, tossed Christopher over his shoulder.

"Where we goin'?" he asked.

Christopher moaned, and the guards laughed uneasily. The younger of the two lupen answered, "There's a transport being readied for Corona."

"We're sending him to the capital?" Creek asked, askance.

"The King wants him," the lupen shrugged. "I guess he wants to get a little revenge on him for everything he did."

Inside the tarp, Christopher listened to them, unable to do anything more. His body was a dizzying mass of pain and spasms, and Creek's shoulder dug painfully into his solar plexus. He almost wished that an incubus could be suffocated, because then the tarp might have been his escape from the misery he was in.

They walked out to the transport, and Christopher could hear the engine noises and the shouts of men and women fulfilling their various duties. His mind was fuzzy and wandering on two different levels, and it almost made the pain more bearable if he could be distracted. One part of him considered the ingenuity of Junko's use of electrocution and alchemical silver, and another part reflected on the use of electrodes during the expressing process that Sebastian had endured. He thought now that he might owe the dragonel and the rest of the Countess's cryptomorphs an apology, if he ever saw any of them again.

It was strange how things had shifted for him so suddenly. The questions that Junko had asked rumbled in his brain, questions about the type and number of cryptomorphs and mythrics in the Community's possession and his own personal sins in service of his so-called science. He wondered how wrong a person could be before they went full circle and started being right again, and he almost laughed at the ridiculousness of that thought. In his professional opinion, he was delirious, and he thought about all of the cryptomorphs that he had seen in this very state. The wheel of justice had turned, grinding him beneath its tread.

The star-shaped brand on his hip throbbed, the signal that the Countess was angry. He wondered if she was angry with him, and if she knew how much he had said, but he dismissed that speculation as paranoia. She was powerful, yes, and she owned him, but that didn't mean that she heard every word that came out of his mouth, every second of every day.

Did it?

Creek dumped him unceremoniously on a cold metal surface, and something was connected to the ties on the tarp that encased him. He supposed he was being tied down to the floor of the transport with bungee cords in much the same way that cryptomorphs were bound to the floor of the Countess's van when she wanted to bring them out to the estate.

He thought about Kiril, the minoton that she had brought to the estate for her amusement in the week before Sebastian was brought into his life. The cross-breed had been a true GenTel creation, bred in the lab and coaxed into life from a human ovum that Christopher had personally fertilized with the semen of a minotaur who had been expressed at Crown Holdings. Kiril had grown up to be a mountain of a man, dark-haired and full of muscles, and he had a truculent nature as well. He had dared to make eye contact with the Countess when she had gone to look at Sebastian, and for his trouble, he had been taken into the van, bound to the floor, and delivered to the Countess's dungeon. When they finally took him back to Crown Holdings, he was a broken shadow of the minoton he had once been.

Christopher regretted that now.

A door slammed, and then he heard footsteps on a metal surface above him. He imagined he'd been bundled into the luggage hold of a passenger bus, and he wondered who was travelling with him, and where they were all going. He was certain that his experience of their destination would be much different than the one the people above him were going to have.

There was a shimmer behind his eyes, and he felt a familiar energy enter the transport. Sebastian. The spiritual fires in his gut, utterly depleted by his suffering, ached for the taste of his dragonel. He tried to reach out mentally, but his telepathy was inactive, affected by the drugs that his birdman torturer had injected into him. He strained to hear Sebastian's voice, but he wasn't talking. Instead, he could hear the steady drone of the ice dragon called Azanel, and though he knew he should have listened to glean some information, he was tired of thinking and tuned him out.

His body was still shaking, pain ravaging his senses. He wondered what sort of sera Junko had injected into him. There had been three injections. The first had short circuited his brain and converted all of his nerve endings to pain receptors, the second had suppressed all of his demonic abilities, and the third... he wasn't sure what the third had done, besides make it impossible for him to lose consciousness, no matter how wretched his suffering became. He wanted the formulae for those drugs. They could be useful. He tried to think of the compounds that might have been used, and the mental exercise was enough to distract him from his body once again, at least for a little while.

SEBASTIAN

SEBASTIAN FOLLOWED Azanel and the uniformed woman into the transport, a beaten-up passenger bus that had been pressed into service for their needs. They had given him a uniform to wear, replacing the T-shirt and jeans from Crown Holdings. It was odd to wear boots after so many weeks of enforced bare feet. He sat and looked out the window, his hands clenched in his lap. The glass reflected his image back to him, and it was like looking at a stranger. His long hair had been pulled back into a silver clasp, and his officer's uniform was emblazoned with a patch bearing an embroidered golden dragon wearing a crown and flexing long claws. Sebastian felt like he should have remembered the insignia, but when he looked at it, his mind was blank. His mind was always blank.

Azanel sat beside him on the seat, occupying the other half of the two-person bench. He sat too close, and Sebastian could only retreat so far into the side of the vehicle. The ice dragon put a hand on his knee, overly familiar.

"You'll see. When we reach Corona and you see the majesty of the city, all of your memories will come rushing back."

Sebastian wasn't as optimistic, and he didn't know what to say. "I hope you're right."

"I know I'm right. You're stronger than anything the Numeans could do to you." Azanel smiled at him, and his eyes were warm. "You're my Mate. I know you better than anyone, and I know that you can beat this."

The headache that had been plaguing him jangled behind his eyes again, and he turned back toward the window. He was surprised to see Cavan Waters trotting across the tarmac to join them. Azanel saw him, too, and he asked in vexation, "What is *he* doing here?"

Cavan stepped up onto the transport and stowed a huge duffel in the overhead bin that ran along the side over the passenger seats. He went to the uniformed woman and spoke to her quietly, and she nodded. The lieutenant sat down in the seat across the aisle from the one that Azanel and Sebastian were occupying.

Azanel sneered, "What brings you here, Waters?"

"General Doz has assigned me to be Commander Goxtli's guard," the young man answered.

"I don't need a guard," Sebastian objected. "I can take care of myself."

"He means that he's to guard the King from you," Azanel guessed.

"Exactly." Cavan nodded. "But I'm sure there won't be any need for that. Will there?"

Sebastian frowned at the tension between his two companions. "What's going on?"

Azanel turned to face the front. "Nothing."

"It doesn't feel like nothing," the dragonel said.

Cavan smiled tightly. "Prince Azanel doesn't care much for me, I guess."

"I don't care for your assignment. It's completely unnecessary, and it could impede the Commander's recovery."

The uniformed woman turned in her seat. "Lt. Waters is here by my request. Until we can ascertain that there are no after effects of His Highness's captivity, we need someone to safeguard his actions."

Azanel argued, "I can…"

The woman's three-layered voice caught his attention. She sounded like three different people speaking at the same time in three different registers, and it was bizarre. She looked human, but obviously she was not. The lowest of the three voices sounded amused. "Someone competent, Your Highness. His Majesty hasn't forgotten who allowed Prince Sebastian to be taken in the first place."

Cavan gave Azanel an amused side-eye, and the ice dragon sputtered, "That was not my fault."

He had told Sebastian a different story, and again the pain

danced behind his eyes. He rubbed his fingertips over his forehead and said, "It was nobody's fault but whoever took me."

"Hunters," the lieutenant supplied.

"Hunters?" the dragonel asked.

"Mercenaries employed by the Five Cities to capture mythrics."

Azanel shook his head. "The Numeans."

Cavan seemed less than convinced. "If you say so."

The transport lurched into motion, and they all rocked in their seats, startled by the sudden, awkward movement of the big vehicle. Azanel turned his back on Cavan and faced Sebastian.

"This is going to be a very long trip," he said. "We should be flying, but Dr. Montez was concerned about how your body would handle the pressures involved, so we're taking the slower means of travel."

Acidic resentment made his neck itch. "How considerate."

"At any rate, Corona is a long way from here, which means we'll be stopping along the way."

Azanel beamed at him, and the expression was dazzling. His teeth were white and even, and his fair peaches-and-cream complexion was flawless. His long hair, white-blond and silky, had been freed from its clasp and framed his face, setting his pale blue eyes off to perfection. Whatever else the ice dragon was, Sebastian had to admit that he was beautiful.

"You're awfully happy for someone who's going to be staying in these roadside stopovers," Cavan said. "Have you seen Badlands hotels? Not up to royal standards."

Azanel kept his back to the human, not favoring him with his attention. He ignored everything that Cavan had said and kept talking to Sebastian. "I hope you don't mind, but I've arranged it so that we'll be in a room together."

Sebastian squinted at Azanel suspiciously. "And if I do mind?"

"You can stay with me," Cavan said. "I should be the one to room with you, anyway, since I'm your guard."

"I wasn't talking to you," Azanel snapped.

"I know. And I wasn't talking to you, either." Cavan leaned forward in his seat so he could look at Sebastian across the ice dragon's body. "It's up to you, Commander."

"I'd prefer to stay alone."

The uniformed woman shook her head. "That is out of the question."

The dragonel took a deep, annoyed breath, then asked, "Not to be rude, but who are you?"

She smiled. "My name is Kliyo," she answered. "I'm King Goxtli's chief herald, and his representative on this trip. My duty is to see you and your companions safely back to the Golden Hall." Sebastian nodded, and she added, "I once served your mother, before her death. It's been my pleasure to be your assistant since then."

He frowned. "Why do I need an assistant?"

"The role of Crown Prince is very demanding, with many royal duties. When you joined the military, many of the less important duties were delegated to me."

"No offense, but if these duties could be delegated to someone else, they couldn't have been that important."

Kliyo's smile widened. "That's what you always said. You always felt that you had better things to do with your time than to attend gallery openings and gala stage performances."

Azanel was watching Sebastian closely. "Does this make you remember anything?"

He sighed. "No."

"Give it time," Cavan advised. "The more you push, the less you'll remember. Just relax and let it come to you."

"No. He should try," the ice dragon objected. "Focus on

the things you remember. Think hard on them, and more memories will come to you."

Sebastian didn't know which approach was better, and he didn't know what to say. Kliyo told the dragonel, "As for accommodations, while it is customary for Mates to share rooms, and I know that Prince Azanel claims Mateship, we can all tell that there's no bond there."

Azanel's face flushed, and the dragonel raised an eyebrow. He offered a plausible excuse, though he didn't know why he did. "It may be that the neural editing disrupted it."

"Or maybe it was never there," Cavan suggested.

Azanel moved so quickly that he was nothing but a blur, and when he stopped, he was standing over Cavan with a blade pressed to the human's throat. Azanel's blue eyes had turned silver and reptilian, and he hissed, "How dare you?!"

Cavan locked his gaze with Azanel's and calmly asked, "That's a neat magic trick. Do you do kids' birthday parties?"

Sebastian went to Azanel and put a hand on his wrist. "Drop the knife," he said softly. "This won't help anything."

"He accuses me of lying," the ice dragon growled. Silver and white iridescent scales sprang into being all along his exposed skin, which had seemed perfectly human before, and claws began to grow from his fingertips.

"Drop. The. Knife."

Azanel looked at Sebastian, then slowly retreated, taking his weapon away from the unimpressed human's neck. Cavan watched as Sebastian coaxed the ice dragon back to their seat, switching sides so that now he was on the aisle while Azanel was pressed against the window.

Sebastian looked at Kliyo and spoke firmly. "I'm staying alone."

She sighed but inclined her head. "As you wish, Your Highness."

In Numea, that refusal would have earned him a thrashing, and probably another round with Lord Ashmar's cane. Sebastian's heart beat quicker, processing the automatic fear of reprisal that washed through him.

No punishment came. He wasn't certain what to think about that.

CHAPTER FIVE

SEBASTIAN

They stopped for the night at what looked like a regular roadside hotel that had fallen on hard times and been abandoned. They were still in the Badlands, so the scrabbly bushes and trees that someone had planted near the lobby doors were baked and half-dead, making the place look even more desolate. The roof had been patched with sheets of corrugated tin, but there were still asphalt roofing tiles in place. Those combined with the peeling paint on the walls showed Sebastian what the hotel had been intended to resemble. He wondered if this had ever been a beautiful place, or if the hotel had always had delusions of grandeur.

As they disembarked, a van pulled up behind them and disgorged four sour-faced uniformed men who busied themselves with the cargo hold of their transport. Sebastian watched them for a moment, then asked Kliyo, "Who are they?"

"Our escort and defense," she answered. "They will stand guard while we sleep."

"Why do we need extra guards? I thought that's why Lt. Waters was here."

She looked at him as if he'd sprouted horns. "You were stolen by Hunters while you were here in the Badlands. Do you want to take the chance of that happening again?"

He frowned. Her words rang true, and this time the headache that normally sprang up when someone spoke of his capture stayed away. "What happened when I was taken?"

Cavan joined them. "Your unit was in the Badlands to rescue Princess Elisa, and you were attacked."

"Princess Elisa?"

"The shadow dragon representative on the Dragon Council," Kliyo explained. "She had been kidnapped and they were taking her back to Numea."

Sebastian turned to Cavan. "Lie to me."

He was taken aback. "What?"

"Lie to me. Tell me a lie. I want to…"

"He's testing his ability," Kliyo told the human. "Do it."

"I've never lied to you in my life," Cavan objected, his voice soft. His expressive blue eyes searched Sebastian's face.

"Then keep it innocuous," the dragonel said. "I'm not asking you to violate any sacred precepts. Am I?"

Cavan smiled. "No. You're not. And I sleep every night with a pink bunny."

The headache stabbed, and Sebastian nodded. "Thank you. Now I know."

Kliyo whispered, "You have the ability to sense the truth."

"Didn't you notice that when you were in Numea?" Cavan asked. "Didn't they ever lie to you there?"

"There were things that were said that made my head feel… jangly," he admitted, "but not the headache that I get here."

"Maybe you were in too much distress from everything

else they were doing that a little headache barely showed up on your radar," the human suggested.

"Maybe."

"Or maybe the closer we get to the Kingdom, the stronger your ability becomes." The middle of her three voices sounded nervous, and she glanced at Azanel, who was directing the guards at the cargo hold.

Sebastian followed her gaze. "Does he know that I'm a truth senser?"

"No." Cavan shifted his grip on his duffel. "He doesn't. And I'd like to keep it that way."

He nodded. "So would I."

"You don't trust him," the human said.

Sebastian answered honestly. "I'm not sure I trust any of you."

"That's fair." He cleared his throat,. "So, briefly, about your capture. Our unit of the Claws…"

"I thought you said we were in the King's Talons." Sebastian connected the words talon and claw as soon as he spoke. "Oh. That's colloquial."

"Right. We call ourselves the Claws. Anyway, our unit was in the Badlands to get Elisa back from the Hunters. We were supposed to have air support from Azanel's squadron, but for whatever reason, the Flying Dragons never came. We thought we were up against a squad of ten Hunters, and that should have been easy, but when we were raiding their camp we got ambushed by a detachment from the Numean army." He ran a hand over his short-cropped hair. "Most of us died. You, Lupul and Mavin were taken. Tilde and I were the only survivors on the ground, and we were both injured."

"Lupul and Mavin?"

"Two of our guys."

"Cryptomorphs?" he asked, trying to understand.

Cavan looked at him strangely. "Mythrics."

Kliyo told him, "The term cryptomorph is for a human/mythric cross, generally one that GenTel Labs cooks up. If there are any cryptomorphs in the Kingdom, they're escapees from that horrible place."

Sebastian nodded. "Was Elisa rescued?"

The human smiled. "Always thinking of the mission, Commander?" he teased. "Yes, we got her home. Barely. The Flying Dragons showed up the next day and took credit for the rescue."

"Technically, they did rescue her," Kliyo told him. "And they also rescued you and Tilde. Prince Azanel is offended by your lack of gratitude."

"They left us to hang and their dereliction of duty allowed the capture to happen in the first place," Cavan said bitterly. "I'm not going to grovel at his feet like he's some kind of savior when twelve of my comrades died because he didn't bother to show his pretty face."

Sebastian understood the animosity between his two companions now. He nodded. "That isn't the story he told me, but he did take responsibility for my capture."

"Why?" Cavan asked. "What did he tell you?"

"That we were at his estate and he sent the guards away," Sebastian answered quietly. "And I remember a lake, and sitting with Azanel on a pier, but the rest..."

Cavan said flatly, "The rest is a lie."

Kliyo looked at the ice dragon, who was approaching with two bags in his hands. "Interesting."

"Why would he lie about that, but still leave himself in a bad light?" Sebastian wondered aloud.

Cavan shrugged. "So you'd understand why people gave him the side-eye from time to time, I guess. Who knows why he does anything?"

Azanel reached them. "Why are we waiting outside? Let's get checked in."

The dragonel looked over Azanel's shoulder and watched the guards wrestling a rolled tarp out of the cargo hold. "What are they doing?"

Azanel glanced back. "Getting their gear. Don't worry about it." He gestured with his bags. "Let's go."

They went into the lobby, which had once had beautiful marble floors and gently fluted columns. Only one of the columns remained, its fellows replaced by steel, and the marble tiles on the floor were broken and chipped. Sebastian could see bullet holes in the walls behind the reception desk, and he stood quietly, wondering what had happened here.

The ice dragon handled the business of getting rooms arranged and paid for, using a chit that bore an insignia that matched the dragon's head on Sebastian's borrowed uniform. Electronic keys were programmed and provided.

"Your room is on the third floor," Azanel told Sebastian. "You're right next to mine. Waters will be on your other side. Don't worry - if anything happens, one or both of us will hear you, and we'll come when you call."

The dragonel took the key. "I'm not going to call, but thank you."

Azanel handed him a bag,. "Clean uniforms and toiletries," he said simply. "In case you wanted to change in the morning."

"Thank you." The bag was heavier than it should have been, and he shifted his grip on the strap. "I'm going to go up to the room."

The desk clerk said, "If you want food, room service is still active for another hour."

Behind them, Kliyo raised her eyebrows, and the highest of her three voices spoke more loudly than the others. "Room service? Out here?"

The clerk blushed. "Well… it's not much, but we do have a rudimentary menu."

Azanel told Sebastian, "We've packed provisions."

Kliyo accepted her key card. "That's a very good thing. Let's get dinner handed out, and then we can get some rest."

~

CHRISTOPHER

CHRISTOPHER WAS THROWN over someone's shoulder, and the shift in position and the indelicate way he was being manhandled awakened the pain in his body all over again. He'd found some relief by lying perfectly still, but now that he was in motion again, the agony was back. He groaned, and someone hit him on the head with something heavy. He fell silent.

The walking turned into stair-climbing, and he heard a door opening with a key card. There was more walking, and then he was dumped unceremoniously onto a bed. The impact with the mattress sent shockwaves through his body, and his shaking intensified.

"Well, I guess it's not dead," an unfamiliar voice said.

"Too bad."

The ropes around his tarp were untied, and the covering was pulled away. He was lying on his back in a filthy hotel room, looking up at a cracked and stained ceiling while Creek pulled the tarp out from beneath him. He rolled onto his side, his body wracked with tremors.

"Fuck," Creek muttered. "He was bleeding all over the tarp."

"So rinse it off in the shower," another of the guards said. It was one of the lupen, and he came closer, looking down at the suffering incubus. "Shit. He looks awful. Do you think he's dying?"

"He'd better not," the other lupen said. Creek disappeared with the tarp, and Christopher could hear water running.

The human guard went to the sink and came back with a damp washcloth. "We have to keep him alive until we get him to the King," he said. "As much as I hate taking care of him, after everything he's done, we really have no choice."

"You're soft, Clayven."

The human frowned. "Whatever."

He sat beside Christopher and wiped the cool cloth over his feverish forehead. It would have felt nice if it weren't for the fact that any touch at all made his pain receptors go into overdrive.

"I don't think I've ever seen anybody tortured like that before," Clayven said, his dark eyes stormy. Christopher looked up at him, and their eyes met. He tried to influence the human, but his abilities failed him, still inaccessible from the injections from his birdman tormentor.

"I don't think I've ever seen anyone who deserved it so much," one of the lupen said. He came to stand at the edge of the bed, leaning over Christopher, grabbing a handful of the incubus's dark hair. He forced Christopher to look at him. "Do I look familiar to you, bitch?"

He tried to speak through cracked lips. "N-no…"

The guard's face twisted. "Just another lupen, huh? Just another piece of meat to be *expressed*?"

"Joro…"

He ignored the human and leaned down, getting right in Christopher's face. "You don't remember me, but I sure as hell remember you." He spat, and an offensive glob of moisture struck the incubus in the eyes. The human guard instantly wiped it away with his cloth.

"Nice," Clayven commented sarcastically. "Leave him alone."

Christopher looked into the lupen's green eyes. "I'm...sorry..."

Joro snorted. "I'll bet you are. Not half as sorry as you're gonna be."

Creek returned, tossing the damp tarp over a dilapidated arm chair in the corner. He sat down on the second of the two beds in the motel room, looking at Christopher, who could only look back.

"How close to dead do you think he is?"

Clayven shrugged. "I don't know. I'm not a medic."

Creek rubbed his own crotch, considering. "I think I'd like to have some fun with him, now that we know he's not gonna enjoy it."

Joro turned away. "You're out of your mind."

"Don't act so high and mighty," Creek taunted. "You're the one who face-fucked him."

"I know, okay?" He crossed the room and went out of Christopher's line of sight. "I'm not proud of it."

The other lupen finally spoke. "It's just part of the inter-rogation process," he said. "We were breaking him down. After everything his people did to us at Crown Holdings, I think it's our right."

The incubus combed through his memory, trying to pull up any recognition of the name Joro, however fleeting. He couldn't remember being involved in the harvesting of speci-mens from any lupen, but there were so many mythrics and crypotomorphs in GenTel's possession that it was hard to say. Even if he personally hadn't taken part in this lupen's suffering, he had been part of the team responsible. He closed his eyes.

"I don't..." He took a breath and marshalled his strength to continue speaking. "... blame you."

Creek punched him in the side of the head, stunning him. Stars danced in Christopher's eyes as the reptilian guard hissed, "Don't you dare fucking forgive us!"

"Bastard," Joro said. "He's ruining everything."

Clayven shook his head and wadded up the cloth, keeping the part with the spittle on it to the inside. He ran the relatively clean portion of the fabric over Christopher's cheek. "It's psychology," he told them. "Remember, this guy's a demon. He knows how to hurt you, and he knows what gets to you."

"If he forgives us for hurting him, there's no point in hurting him more," Creek fumed.

"He knows that."

Joro snorted. "Clever, and sort of badass, to still be playing mind games with us in the shape he's in."

Christopher sighed. "No… mind games."

The human guard left his side, and Joro sat down where he had been. "See, that's the thing. I don't believe a word out of your mouth. Everything you say is a fucking lie."

"Not… everything…."

Clayven spoke from the area near the sink. "Leave him alone right now. We've got to get him to the King, and if we do anything to him, he might not live."

"He'll live," grumbled the deep-voiced lupen, the one whose name Christopher hadn't heard. "Demons are hard to kill, and this one is going to stay alive just to spite us. He's probably trying to work out how he's going to escape. This helpless act is just that: an act."

Christopher laughed feebly, and to his own ears, he sounded unhinged. Joro stood up and walked away in disgust, and Creek stormed to the door.

"I'm gonna get some ice," the reptilian said, seizing a plastic bucket on his way past the nightstand.

"Ice? In this dump?" Joro mocked. "This isn't Corona. This joint barely has water, let alone ice!"

"There was water," Creek pointed out. "Besides, this motel was picked by the ice dragon. He wouldn't stop someplace where his pretty self would have to do without."

The door opened and slammed shut, and Christopher could sense the shift in energy in the room. Now there were only three guards with him. Apparently Creek had gone on his stated expedition.

Christopher opened his eyes and looked at Joro, who was pacing not far away. The room was small, so there really wasn't far that he could go. "Where is… Seb…astian?"

"The prince is here, in the hotel," Clayven answered. "But don't think for a minute we're going to let you anywhere near him."

Joro agreed. "Yeah. You've done enough damage."

The second lupen, the one with the deep voice, left the room as well, and Christopher could sense his lifeforce walking away. He wished that he could pull some of the ambient energy out of the air. Perhaps it would help him recover. Like his telepathy and mesmerism, though, that ability had been hampered by the injections. He sighed.

Clayven came to him with a plastic cup filled with lukewarm water. He helped Christopher sit up, and the incubus cried out in pain as he was moved.

"Shut up," the human guard told him. "Drink this."

He accepted, grateful for the liquid. He swallowed the few sips that Clayven allowed him before he dumped him on the bed again.

"That's the extent of my medical ability," the human told his companion.

Joro sat down on the other bed, and from where he was lying, Christopher could study him. The longer he looked at him, the longer he was convinced that he had never even examined this lupen. He wasn't guilty of anything where Joro was concerned, at least not on a personal level, but he supposed that group guilt was sufficient to merit punishment.

He closed his eyes and tried to breathe normally, a feat that was made more difficult by the intermittent spasms of his body. The shaking was making him nauseated, and he regretted the water he had drunk.

It was going to be a long, long night.

CHAPTER SIX

SEBASTIAN

Sebastian slept alone that night, his door locked and bolted and a chair shoved under the doorknob to keep out any interlopers. The last time he had been alone to sleep had been in the shed on the Countess's estate, a filthy place where he'd been held pending his debut at her dinner party. When he closed his eyes, he could practically feel the collar around his neck, just barely loose enough to let him breathe, connected to the ceiling by a chain. He had been placid then in ways he couldn't comprehend, but now the thought of being chained like a dog was demeaning and infuriating.

It took him hours to fall asleep, but when the darkness was deepest, he managed to slide away. His dreams were turbulent, but the only things he remembered when he woke were images of storm clouds and the sound of screaming.

The hotel had a continental breakfast, and the Kingdom's forces helped themselves to stale bagels and runny scrambled eggs before heading back out to the transport. The wind was picking up, blowing hot across the sandy ground, sending grit up into their eyes as they walked out of the building.

Kliyo covered her eyes with goggles and wrapped a scarf tightly around her neck, guarding herself from the blowing dust. Sebastian's scales were unaffected, but the rest of his skin felt scoured.

The guards were wrestling their tarp-covered parcel into the cargo hold again, most of its weight carried over the shoulder of the largest guard, a reptilian with green-gray skin. The burden was bent strangely over the guard's back, and as he moved it, the bundle shifted. Sebastian suddenly realized that they were carrying a person, or at least a live being, in that tarp.

"Hey!" he shouted. "Hold up! What are you doing?"

Azanel put a hand on his arm. "Ignore them…"

"No." He pulled away and walked quickly toward the guards, who had hesitated uncertainly. Cavan fell into step beside him. "I said, what are you doing?"

"Uh…" One of the other guards, a human with a sallow and sickly complexion, glanced at Cavan. "We're loading up."

Sebastian frowned. "Put that down."

The guards looked at Azanel, who shook his head, but Cavan stepped up to stand at Sebastian's side and said, "You heard the prince. Put it down."

Reluctantly, they did. A groan escaped from beneath the wrappings, and Sebastian knew that voice. He rushed forward and tore the ropes away, exposing Christopher's naked and shaking form. He was leaking blood from a hundred puncture wounds, and his eyes were entirely black. The only time he had seen Christopher's eyes that way had been in the basement of the Countess's estate when Lord Ashmar had been beating him. From what little he knew, those black eyes were a sign that Christopher was in desperate pain. Sebastian's chest tightened with concern and anger.

The incubus looked up at him and croaked, "Hi."

"What the actual fuck?!" Cavan exploded. "You've been carrying a prisoner like cargo? This is outrageous!"

"We were ordered…" the reptilian guard began.

"By who?" Cavan demanded.

"By me." Azanel stepped forward. "Do you know who this is, Lt. Waters?"

"It's a demon, but that doesn't excuse this behavior."

The ice dragon squinted against the wind and told him, "This is Christopher Balika, the Oppressor."

Cavan's eyes narrowed, and the muscles in his jaw jumped. "The one who had Commander Goxtli in his custody."

"The one who was using him as a sex slave," Azanel growled. Sebastian flushed in shame. "Does that change your opinion on his treatment?"

Cavan looked at Sebastian, then at the ice dragon. "No. It doesn't matter what he's done. The Kingdom is better than this."

"He isn't what you think." Sebastian put his hand under Christopher's head. "Can you move?"

The incubus' body twisted, wracked with muscle spasms. Where Sebastian was touching him, he could feel electrical currents coursing through his flesh. Tears sprang into his eyes.

"What have they done to you?"

The reptilian guard tried again. "We were…"

Cavan snapped, "Don't tell me you were ordered. I don't fucking care."

"What is in him?" Sebastian asked, looking up at Azanel accusingly.

The ice dragon admitted, "I don't know. I wasn't privy to his interrogation."

"*Interrogation*," Sebastian spat. "Torture!"

"Like he tortured you?"

Christopher closed his eyes and writhed again, gritting his teeth around an anguished groan. Cavan clicked his tongue and knelt on his other side, facing Sebastian and turning his back on the guards, who were backing away in guilty confusion, unable to comprehend why the dragonel was defending their prisoner. He turned the incubus onto his side and held his trembling hands over Christopher's body.

"What are you doing?" Sebastian asked.

"Shh."

As he watched, hundreds of tiny, shining metallic pellets backed themselves out of the bleeding wounds in Christopher's body. Cavan closed his eyes, perspiration dotting his face, and his hands trembled more quickly. The pellets lifted away from the incubus and gathered in the air, hovering there until Cavan gestured sharply. The little bits of metal scattered across the rocky ground. They sparked with electricity, blue arcs of power connecting them to one another where they lay.

Immediately, Christopher's many wounds healed shut, and he let out a long sigh of relief, sagging into Sebastian's hand, which still cupped his head. Sebastian stroked his hair and looked at Cavan.

"How...?"

"I'm a witch." He stood and wiped his hands on his uniform trousers, shaky and clearly exhausted.

Christopher opened his eyes, which had returned to their normal limpid brown. "Thank you."

"I didn't do that for you," Cavan answered harshly. "I will not be party to torture, and this is a violation of everything the Kingdom stands for."

The incubus laughed cynically. "You don't know your Kingdom very well."

"Like you do?" Cavan scoffed.

"Shut him up," Azanel growled.

Sebastian helped Christopher sit up, servile and solicitous and not knowing why. "Can we get him some clothes? Give him some dignity."

"Like the dignity he gave you?" Azanel demanded.

"That's not…"

He interrupted Sebastian, "That *is* important. You were mistreated, and it burns me to my core to know that the one who did it is lying here now. I want to kill him for what he did."

The dragonel pulled Christopher close, protecting him. "Don't you dare!"

Cavan rolled his eyes. "Good Goddess, this is a mess."

Kliyo nodded. "Indeed." She nodded to the guards. "You heard the prince. Why must his orders to you always be repeated? Give the prisoner something to wear."

One of the lupen guards, his face sour, went into the hotel while Sebastian said, "He is not going back into the cargo hold. He's going to ride in the transport, in a seat like the rest of us."

"Fine," Azanel snarled. "But I demand that he remain manacled."

Christopher nodded to Sebastian, who acquiesced. "Fine."

The look Cavan was giving Sebastian was a combination of concern, disappointment and irritation, but he said nothing. Azanel was less reticent about his opinion.

"He still controls you," he accused. "You still have feelings for this… this *monster*."

"He's not a monster," the dragonel argued. "You don't know him the way I do. He's been just as forced to do the things he's done as the rest of us were. He's not a bad person. He's just… a product of his environment. He cared for me when nobody else did, and…" He stopped talking, uncertain how or if to proceed, not even sure if he himself believed what he was saying. He repeated, "You don't know him."

"We only know him by his deeds," Cavan said softly, "but you're right - he should be in the transport. He's still a sentient being, and I wouldn't put a dog in the cargo hold."

The lupen returned with a pair of trousers and a T-shirt, both of which were oversized on Christopher when he put them on. Sebastian was glad that the incubus was at least clothed properly. He knew that he had always felt better when he could be dressed instead of naked while he was in captivity.

He helped Christopher to his feet. "Can you stand?"

The incubus nodded, even though he leaned into Sebsatian. "I'm all right now."

"Liar."

Kliyo looked at her watch, then cleared her throat. The lowest of her three voices carried more clearly than the others as she said, "We have to go. Get on board, please. Time is wasting."

They went onto the transport, and Christopher was handcuffed with each wrist attached to the metal bar forming part of the back of the seat ahead of him. Sebastian sat beside him.

"Sebastian," the ice dragon chided softly. "Come up here with me."

"I'll sit here, thank you." He glanced at Christopher, then back at Azanel. "It's my choice, I believe."

"It is," Kliyo allowed, "but we might prefer it if you put more distance between yourself and your captor."

"I would prefer it if I didn't."

He was not going to budge on the point, and the others could tell. Azanel sat down with a disgusted sigh, and Kliyo shrugged, turning in her seat to face the front. Cavan sat across the aisle from Sebastian.

"I don't need a guard," the dragonel told him.

"That remains to be seen."

Christopher sighed. "I'm not going to do anything to him, I swear. Even if I wanted to, I can't. My powers have all been shut down."

Cavan raised one eyebrow but said nothing.

They rode in silence for a long time, the air heavy with unspoken words. Sebastian finally turned to Christopher and whispered to him, "Are you still hurting?"

"No. Your witch friend is very good at what he does."

"Who did this to you?"

He shrugged, as if the situation were minor and unimportant. "An avian mythric named Junko, on the orders of your troglodyte officer."

"Not my officer," Sebastian corrected quietly.

Christopher's dark eyes searched his face. "Do you remember any of them?"

He glanced up at the back of Azanel's head and whispered, "No."

"But do you feel at home?"

"No." Sebastian met his gaze and said, "I'm not at home anywhere."

"Not even with me?"

It was difficult for him to interpret Christopher's tone, and he felt caught between what he wanted to say and what he thought the required answer might have been. He didn't want to make an error and possibly have to pay for it later. He shook his head at himself. He was no longer in the Countess's custody, and no longer subject to the Community and their brutal rules. He no longer wore the collar they'd put him in; why did he keep acting as if he did?

He chose honesty. "Nowhere."

Christopher nodded sadly. "I understand."

"Do you?" Sebastian asked, taking a risk and challenging his Master, who was his Master no longer. He had to find a way to remember that. The stress of his warring impulses made him snappish. "Do you really?"

"I... " He took a breath. "I can't say that I've ever been in your exact position, with no memories left, but I do know what it's like to be torn out of my home and thrown into a situation you don't understand."

With a disgusted noise, Cavan rose and rummaged through the overhead compartment, then distributed bottles of water to everyone in the transport. He handed two to Sebastian.

"You both should stay hydrated. The Badlands are arid."

Christopher gestured with his hands, unnecessarily reminding them of his handcuffs, which would prevent him from lifting the bottle to his lips. Sebastian said, "I'll help you."

He held the bottle so that the incubus could drink, and Cavan turned away with an annoyed expression, then took out a tablet and started to read. The dragonel didn't understand how the soldier who claimed to be his friend could be compassionate one minute and then disdainful of Sebastian's compassion the next. He didn't understand the people around him at all.

When Sebastian lowered the bottle, Christopher smiled gratefully. "Thank you."

"You're welcome."

Azanel glanced back once, then turned away. The cabin settled into uncomfortable silence for the rest of the ride to the next hotel.

As the transport rolled on, Christopher began to nod off, exhausted from his ordeal. Because of the handcuffs, he could only lean forward to rest his head against his hands, forcing him into a position that must have been uncomfortable. He turned his face toward Sebastian, avoiding the light that streamed in through the window beside him.

To Sebastian, the slumbering Christopher looked gentle and almost angelic. He wanted to kiss his soft lips, but he held back, both to keep from waking his former Master and to prevent himself from giving in to his emotions.

He was confused about what he was feeling, uncertain what was real and what was manufactured by someone else. He had been in the Countess's custody for a year. That was a long time for them to mess with his mind, and the brief memories he had made it all too clear that they were only too happy to abuse him in every way they could. Christopher had been party to that abuse, and he wondered how many times they'd encountered one another, and what memories of Christopher he had lost. Did he truly love him? How could he, after everything that had happened?

He wanted to believe that his heart was his own, and that he was able to choose for himself whom he loved and whom he accepted into his bed and into his body. At the same time, he knew that he had been conditioned to be passive, accepting, docile. From what he gathered, docile was something that the real him had never been, if the people from the Kingdom were to be believed. But what memories of them had he lost? And was he finally among friends, or had he simply stumbled into another kind of captivity?

The uncertainty was choking. Sebastian closed his eyes and took a deep, calming breath. Across the aisle, Cavan asked him quietly, "Are you okay?"

He looked over at the witch and smiled sadly. "No. Not really."

Cavan shifted so he could face Sebastian more fully. "I can only imagine how hard this is for you."

He gave a short, melancholy laugh. "No, I don't think you can."

Cavan smiled. "Well... probably not. But I've been thinking and putting myself in your shoes, and it sucks so hard. I think you're incredibly strong to not be rocking in a corner right now."

"Thank you, I think."

"Seriously. I'm not going to lie… I'm not sure how you can be so forgiving of him, after the breeding program and the torture and the mind control…" He shook his head. "I'd hate him. I do hate him."

Sebastian narrowed his eyes. "I never said anything about any mind control."

"Mind wiping? That's not mind control?"

His head twinged. "You're lying."

Cavan looked surprised, then sighed. "Okay. You're right. I didn't find out about it from you. I found out about it from him."

"How?"

Cavan handed him the tablet he'd been reading. "This is his confession."

Anger flashed through Sebastian, and the red glow behind his scales briefly illuminated the back of the seat ahead of him. "The one they tortured him into giving?"

"Yeah."

"Confessions under torture are questionable."

"Sometimes, but this one? He gave chapter and verse." He gestured toward the screen, which was currently black and inert. "You might find it interesting. It might even jog some memories."

Sebastian put the tablet aside. "You said that we were close. Were we good friends?"

Cavan nodded, his blue eyes serious. He retrieved the tablet. "Very good."

"Then why don't I remember you at all? When I look at your face, you're not at all familiar to me. I don't know you."

The witch winced but tried to hide it. "I know. Do you know anybody here?"

He looked around at the other passengers. "I have a few broken memories of Azanel. But that's all."

Cavan nodded again. "I see."

"Do you?"

He smiled crookedly. "No, but I want to. Look, Sebastian, I'm trying to be as patient and as understanding as I can. But this isn't easy for me, either... although what I've got to go through is nothing compared to your burden. I know that."

Christopher stirred, and the dragonel looked at him. The incubus's dark eyes flickered open, and Cavan, seeing that Christopher was awake, sighed and straightened in his seat to look straight ahead. Sebastian put a hand on his seat mate's shoulder.

"Are you feeling better?" he asked.

"Marginally." He straightened and stretched his neck. "Wow... I've got such a kink."

Cavan snorted. "We know."

Sebastian tossed a brief glare in Cavan's direction, then turned back to Christopher. "Are you in any pain?"

"Some aching, but nothing bad. Thanks." He looked into Sebastian's eyes. "Are you all right?"

He gave the only answer that he could think of. "No."

CHAPTER SEVEN

SEBASTIAN

They reached their next stopover well after dark, and Azanel and Kliyo went to the front desk to make arrangements while the guards none too gently unshackled Christopher from the seat and cuffed his hands behind his back. The hotel where they had stopped was in better shape than the last, which indicated to Sebastian that they were getting closer to the border of the Kingdom. They were still in the Badlands, still passing through endless expanses of blighted soil and scrub, but there was more foliage now. Sebastian wondered if the Kingdom was verdant and fertile, and if its greenery extended out into the Badlands near the border.

Azanel returned with the keys. He held one out to Sebastian and said, "I would like it if you would stay with me, but I think I know that you intend to be with *him*."

"You're right." He took the key.

"You can't trust him," the ice dragon warned. "If you're alone with him, he'll seduce you, or he'll activate whatever triggers they implanted into your brain and make you obedient to him again."

The thought of once more submitting to Christopher was more exciting than it should have been, and Sebastian tried to conceal his response to the images his mind supplied. "What are you afraid of? That I'll set him free?"

"Honestly, I'm afraid that you'll take him and run back to Numea."

Sebastian snorted. "Oh, believe me. I'm never going back there."

Azanel looked relieved. "I'm happy to hear that."

He glanced at Christopher, who was standing quietly, flanked by the guards. The reptilian was hissing at him, but the incubus looked unimpressed. He turned back to Azanel. "If you're concerned, put a guard outside my door."

The dragon looked surprised. "You'd allow that?"

"If it would allay your fears, yes."

Azanel beckoned to Cavan, who joined them. "Lt. Waters, the prince has decided that he will keep the prisoner in his room tonight."

Cavan's deep blue eyes flicked to Sebastian's face, then away again. "Really."

"Yes. And I have decided that you should stand guard outside the door to listen for any distress, or to apprehend the Oppressor if he tries to escape."

Cavan drew himself up to his full height, which wasn't quite equal to Azanel's. "You're not my commander."

Azanel smiled. "No, but don't you want to ensure that your prince is safe?"

"Of course I do." He glanced at Christopher. "All right. I'll do it. But as his Mate, don't you want to ensure his safety, too?" He leaned on the word 'Mate" with sarcasm, and Sebastian looked at Azanel for a reaction.

The dragon scowled. "You know I do."

"Then maybe we should split the night. You take one

shift, I'll take the next. Then we're both awake for the arrival in Corona."

"That's a brilliant idea," Sebastian said. "You should do that."

Christopher snickered, and Azanel strode over to him, silencing him with a heavy blow to the jaw. The incubus's head snapped to the side and staggered back a few steps. He straightened and looked at Azanel with amusement.

"Is that all you've got?"

The ice dragon sneered and shifted into a half-dragon version of himself, his eyes silver and his scales shining in the light from the motel sign. He took a threatening step toward Christopher, and Sebastian stopped him with a hand on his chest.

"Please don't."

Azanel looked at Sebastian, betrayed, then turned and stalked away. Cavan called after him, "So, you'll take second watch, right?" The ice dragon took a moment to flip him off, and the witch laughed.

Sebastian walked to the reptilian guard. "I need the keys to his manacles."

The guard looked startled, and the dragonel wasn't certain if it was because he had spoken to him, or because of the nature of the request. He looked from Sebastian to Azanel's retreating back. "I…" He swallowed. "Right."

The guard dug into his pocket and pulled out the electronic key to the handcuffs. Sebastian took it and considered losing it permanently. "Thank you."

"Yes, sir."

He looked at the number on the key card and then walked back to Christopher. "We're on the bottom floor, which is lucky," he said.

"Lucky? Why?" Cavan asked.

"Because I think the floor outside the rooms upstairs

might fall apart." It was a pretty lie, and his head ached when he said it. Cavan looked less than convinced. He took Christopher's elbow in his hand. "This way."

The incubus pulled free of his grip without rancor and walked quietly beside him to the hotel room whose number was on the key. Cavan followed at a discreet distance. Sebastian opened the door, and he and his former Master stepped inside.

The room was shabby but mostly clean, give or take some cobwebs in the corners and a stain on the carpet near the corner. Sebastian locked the door and tossed the key onto the night stand.

"Turn around," he told Christopher, who obeyed. He unlocked the handcuffs and tossed them on the floor, mimicking the way the incubus had freed him from his collar back in Numea.

Christopher brought his hands around to the front of his body and rubbed at his wrists, where red marks testified to the tightness of the cuffs. "Thank you."

Sebastian sat down on the bed and looked up at Christopher. "Are you all right?"

He smiled crookedly. "Better now that you're here."

The incubus stepped forward, moving to stand in front of Sebastian, his knees between the dragonel's. He finger-combed Sebastian's long blond hair, looking down at him with warmth in his dark eyes.

"Did they hurt you?"

Sebastian thought about the knock-out gas that Dr. Montez had used on him, but he decided not to talk about it. "No. I'm sorry that they hurt you."

Christopher spoke softly, his eyes slightly averted from Sebastian's gaze. A lock of his dark hair fell onto his forehead, charmingly disordered for once. He had always been pin-neat back in Numea. "Do you feel any loyalty to them?"

He shook his head, and the incubus's scarred hands, for once not clad in gloves, cupped the dragonel's face. He could feel energy throbbing in the incubus's palms. He took a deep breath and admitted his confusion.

"No. I don't think so." He took a breath. "I'm not sure if I'm loyal to anybody right now."

"Not even to me?"

Perhaps it was because of Azanel's arch warnings, or maybe it was just an expression of his own uncertainty, but he heard something in Christopher's tone that sounded manipulative. He took the brunet's hands in his own and pulled them away from his cheeks.

"I don't know," he admitted. "I don't know if what I feel is what I feel, or what you made me feel."

"Does it matter?"

Their eyes met, and Sebastian looked away, conscious that the incubus had exercised his mind control through their locked gazes before. Christopher took his chin in his hand and gently made him look at him again.

"I can't affect your mind," he told the dragonel. "I can't use any of my abilities. They took them away from me." There was genuine bitterness in Christopher's tone, and Sebastian felt a sympathetic twinge. He knew what it was to be deprived of a part of himself. The incubus continued. "You don't trust me."

Sebastian stood and walked a few feet away, putting some breathing room between them. "Do you blame me?"

"Honestly? No." His answer surprised Sebastian, and he turned back toward him. "I know that I've done awful things, both in general and specifically to you. All I can do is ask you to forgive me, because…I truly love you."

He thought back to the Countess's estate and the party where Christopher's powers made him perform a live sex show for a group of dinner guests, and about the brutality he'd suffered at the hands of Lord Ashmar that Christopher had promised to prevent but didn't. He also thought of the care the incubus doctor - *veterinarian*, he reminded himself - had shown after Sebastian had been injured. But Christopher had kept him prisoner, and had been part of the breeding program that treated sentient beings like livestock. The dichotomy left his head spinning, and he sat heavily in the single armchair in the room.

"I don't know if I can forgive you. I know I can't forgive the Countess or the Community." He looked up in anguish. "There are eight babies that they stole from me, and I will never see them. Ever. And I don't know how many more they'll make. They took so many samples...Do you know how many times they hooked me up to that damned machine? Do you know how much they took from me?"

Christopher nodded solemnly. "I know. I helped to catalogue it."

Sebastian rose and stalked back across the room toward Christopher. Anger roared through him, and he felt his skin heating, the red glow beginning to back-light his scales again. He pushed Christopher roughly, and the incubus fell backward to sit on the bed, surprised.

"You treated me like an animal! You and your Community and your grandmother and your fucking GenTel Corporation... I am *not* an animal! None of us are! And you had *no right!*"

He stood over the incubus, trembling in his rage, and Christopher looked up at him with tears in his eyes. "I know," he whispered. "And I am so sorry."

"That's not good enough."

"What else can I do?" Christopher asked plaintively. "My powers have been stripped from me. I'm all alone here. I'm at the mercy of your Kingdom forces, and they're going to kill me as soon as we get to Corona. Sebastian, this is the last night we're ever going to have. Do you really want to spend it fighting?"

He grabbed Christopher by the throat and pushed him down onto the mattress, straddling him. The incubus stared up at him, his eyes wide and his pupils blown. Sebastian squeezed until the other man's face turned red.

"How do you like it? This is what it's like to have that collar on, to be choked by something that could kill you at any moment. This is what it's like to be completely at someone else's mercy," he growled. *"How do you like it?"*

Christopher mouthed his answer, unable to put any air behind the words. "I… love it…"

Sebastian let go, allowing him to breathe again, confounded, confused and aroused. He could feel Christopher's erection nudging him, and he hesitated, frozen in uncertainty. The incubus sat up and grasped Sebastian by the back of the neck, pulling him into a passionate kiss. Sebastian allowed it, opening his mouth to admit Christopher's tongue. He closed his eyes tightly and grabbed the other man's dark hair in both hands, holding him tightly.

They kissed until both of them were breathless. The incubus pulled away and panted, "Make love with me. Love me and let me love you. Please. We'll never have this chance again."

He shook his head, his eyes still closed. He was afraid, but he wanted what the incubus was offering. He didn't know if this was Christopher trying to re-establish control over him, or if this was real. If tonight was his last chance, though, he couldn't let it go. That would be a regret he'd never stop feeling.

Sebastian opened his eyes and reached down, pulling up the T-shirt that Christopher wore. The incubus helped him pull off the garment and toss it aside. He looked down at the brunet, running his hands over the smooth muscular planes of his torso. He could not deny that Christopher was beautiful, and feelings of intermingled love and lust rushed through him again. He sat back and rubbed against the brunet's cock, a hard and needy bulge inside his borrowed trousers, and Sebastian felt his own cock hardening in response.

He straightened and took off his own shirt T-shirt and threw it on the pillow. Christopher's hands gripped his waist, and then he sat up to mouth the hard paps on Sebastian's chest. Shivers of pleasure ran through him, and he sighed, "Oh, yes."

Christopher palmed him through his jeans, and Sebastian thrust against his hand, letting the incubus feel his need. Dark eyes flickered up toward him, and the dragonel undid the button holding his jeans closed. Christopher reached inside, freeing his cock from its confinement and stroking it gently.

He enjoyed his partner's touch for a long moment, his head tipped back, before he gently pushed his hands away. Sebastian unbuttoned Christopher's trousers and left the bed so he could pull the clothing away, laying the incubus naked before him. He tossed the rest of his own clothing to the floor and rejoined him, seizing his mouth in another desperate kiss.

Christopher opened his legs to him, silently issuing an invitation,and Sebastian settled between his thighs, their cocks lying side by side. He thrust slowly, the motion dragging their sensitive flesh against each other, the friction a source of dizzying delight. Christopher took them both in his hand, holding their cocks together as Sebastian rocked his hips.

"I want you to fuck me," Christopher breathed. "And then I want to fuck you."

"It's not about what you want. Not anymore."

The incubus looked surprised, but Sebastian smiled and adjusted his seat, moving to kneel with his legs around Christopher's narrow waist. The head of the incubus's cock, wet with pre-cum, nudged his opening.

"You're dry," Christopher objected. "Don't make me hurt you."

Sebastian spat into his hand and rubbed the moisture over Christopher's cock, then repeated the action to wet his own hole, his gaze locked to the brunet's the entire time. Christopher's fair cheeks were flushed and his eyes were bright with his desire, and if this was truly the last time he would ever see him this way, Sebastian wanted to remember it.

He pressed down, and Christopher's cock slid inside him. He moaned as he was stretched and filled, and the friction was a bit too much, but he didn't stop until he had taken everything that the incubus had to give. The head of his cock nudged against Sebastian's pleasure spot, and he swiveled his hips, amplifying the feeling. Christopher gasped and grasped the dragonel's thighs.

"Look at me," Sebastian said, slowly rising and falling along Christopher's length. He could feel heat spreading through his chest again, but this time it wasn't the bright red fire of anger. Without the suppressant in his system, he was feeling his body's natural reactions, and the passion inside him glowed golden around his scales.

Christopher shook his head. "You're the most beautiful thing I've ever seen."

Sebastian smiled and bent to kiss him. The incubus caught the dragonel's nipples in his fingertips, rolling them and giving them a gentle tweak. Sparkles flashed down Sebastian's torso, golden glittering that followed the shiver of delight that Christopher's ministrations were making him feel.

He pressed his hands against Christopher's chest and started to ride him in earnest, fucking himself on the long cock that filled him so deliciously. He was leaking pre-cum onto Christopher's abdomen, and the incubus dabbled a finger in the sticky fluid before he brought it to his mouth so he could taste it. His gaze never faltered, and Sebastian tried to read the things he saw there but failed. His own emotions were intense and muddled, and he wanted the moment to last forever, Christopher buried in his body, his own cock rubbing against his lover's warm skin.

"Christopher," he moaned. "I need you."

Breathlessly, he answered, "You have me."

The pleasure was too intense to last. Sebastian let loose, unable to contain himself, spurting onto Christopher's tight abdomen. The incubus began to thrust up into him, and only a minute later he was bathing Sebastian's insides with his hot cum, a ragged cry ripping from his throat.

They rode out their orgasms until they had to separate, and Sebastian reluctantly let Christopher slide back out of him. He lay down at the incubus's side and kissed him tenderly, his hand in the incubus's dark hair.

"This is not our last night," he promised him. "Not by a long shot."

A look of deep sorrow filled Christopher's face, and he whispered, "You might not have a say in the matter."

He pulled his lover close and held him in his arms, feeling sleepy and sated. "I won't let them hurt you," he swore, though a part of him wondered if he would be able to keep his promise.

Christopher turned in his arms so they could spoon, and Sebastian kissed his shoulders. For the first time, he saw the white lines of old scars, and he touched them with a gentle hand.

"Lord Ashmar?" he asked.

Christopher sighed. "Who else? The Countess's personal torturer."

His dark eyes glanced down toward his body, and he took Sebastian's hand, pressing his palm to the star-shaped brand on his hip. Sebastian could feel it throbbing, surprised by the amount of heat that it emitted.

Quietly, the incubus said, "This is the only scar she's ever put on me, but it connects me to her. If she wants to, she can track me with it, or sense what I'm doing."

Sebastian frowned. "Does she keep tabs of you all the time?"

"Not all the time. Right now she's looking."

A flash of mischief coursed through him. "Do you think she knows that we just made love?"

Christopher chuckled. "I have no idea. If she does, she must be very annoyed."

"Good," Sebastian smiled, kissing the incubus's neck. "Let's annoy her again…"

CHAPTER EIGHT

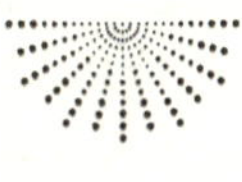

CAVAN

Cavan stood outside the hotel room door, leaning against the wall with his arms crossed. Inside, he could hear Christopher and Sebastian. When they were arguing, he was tempted to go inside and break it up, but it was Sebastian's voice that was raised, and he figured that if any one had the right to yell a little, it was the dragonel.

The sounds changed to something much more personal, and he tried not to listen. He knew that Sebastian and the demon had been sexual partners in Numea, and he knew that for incubi, seduction was their stock in trade. Though listening to the two men making love was deeply uncomfortable for him, he listened for sounds of distress from his prince. He heard none, and so he stayed outside, waiting, grateful that he had been the one on guard duty and not Azanel.

He didn't trust the ice dragon, and to say that he was skeptical of Azanel's claims was an understatement. Allegedly, before their unit's ill-fated raid on the Badlands, Azanel and Sebastian had spent the weekend together at the ice dragon's country estate. If he was to be believed, he and

Sebastian had spent those summer days together in a lover's swoon, bonding and Mating and exchanging their vows of eternal love.

Cavan didn't buy it.

For one thing, he knew that Sebastian was not the swoony, love-swearing type, or at least had never been before. He also knew that Azanel was not the romantic that he claimed to be. In the year after his return from the Badlands, Cavan had taken it upon himself to investigate Azanel's claims, and he had learned some interesting things.

While he'd been recovering from the wounds he'd received in the raid, he'd taken a position as a guard in the Dragon Council's meeting chambers. Dragons were spectacularly mercurial and arrogant. They believed that their tongue was too special to be spoken by anyone without their blood, and that they were too superior to the rest of the cryptids and mythrics in the Kingdom for anyone to question what they did. They spoke freely to one another in their mother tongue as long as the King was absent, no matter who was in attendance.

The Council members, one from each dragon tribe, had frank and treasonous discussions about the King and his heir apparent, Sebastian. They hadn't troubled themselves with discretion. Cavan was just a human, after all, or so he appeared. They failed to realize that he was a witch, and forgot that draconic was the language of elemental magic. Perhaps other witches were content to cast their spells and conduct their rituals in the common tongue, but Cavan was the seventh son of a seventh son, and he'd been taught more of the classical ways of his people. He spoke draconic like a native speaker, more or less. There were some sounds he couldn't exactly replicate due to the different physiology of his throat, but that just meant he had an accent. He understood everything they said.

The Council did not approve of King Goxtli. He was the third golden dragon to sit upon the throne, which was two golden kings too many as far as the rest of the Council was concerned. The Golden Throne was supposed to rotate through the dragon tribes, but the golds had kept and held it for centuries. King Goxtli had taken an ifrit as his Mate, and they had produced a half-breed child, Sebastian. It vexed the dragons, especially the representative of the shadow dragons, that a half-dragon, half-fire elemental would be inheriting the throne. The Dragon Council were not Sebastian's friends, and Azanel was part of the Council as the representative of the ice tribe.

Cavan didn't believe that Azanel's interest in Sebastian was loving or at all pure. He believed that the ice dragon was jockeying for position, trying to elevate his tribe among the other dragon tribes of the Kingdom by marrying into the royal family. If Azanel became Prince Consort when Sebastian inherited the throne, then the ice dragons would be ascendant, supplanting the silver tribe as the second most powerful, and the ones poised to take the throne if the dynasty of golds should falter.

Having a dragonel crown prince was all the faltering that the golden dynasty could bear. There would be no fourth golden dragon king, especially not if Azanel was positioned to take the throne away from his weak so-called Mate.

Cavan knew Sebastian. He had known him for years, and they had been closer than any two men could have been. He doubted that Sebastian would have accepted Azanel as his Mate. The story didn't even come out until Sebastian was captured. The ice dragon had spun his yarn to the heartbroken king, who had been desperate for any news of his missing son. For a year, he hung on Azanel's every word, believing that the ice dragon could confirm his son's well being through the mysteries of their Mating bond. Every day, the king would check with Azanel, asking if his son was still alive. Every day, the ice dragon became more and more indispensable to Goxtli, much to the annoyance of the rest of the court. Goxtli showered him with riches and with praise, heaped honors about his feet, and made Azanel his obvious royal favorite. Nobody dared to move against him.

Azanel claimed that the Mate bond with Sebastian would help him find the dragonel. Cavan had no such esoteric tie, but he did have excellent instincts, a knowledge of the way the League of Five Cities, also called Pentepolis, operated. He also had a better-than-average understanding of the workings of GenTel. He tried to infiltrate the organization to find Sebastian, and once he had come very close, locating the exact farm where the dragonel was being kept. Unfortunately, when he arrived, Sebastian had already seen fit to spring himself from his captivity, at least in the short term. They'd missed one another by a matter of days. Cavan was exposed and had to return to the Kingdom before he was killed, choosing to live and search for Sebastian another day. The dragonel was captured and taken to GenTel, where he was mind-wiped and re-inserted into the obscenity that was the Community's breeding program.

He should have stayed away, but his orders - both from General Doz and his own desires - led him to go back. He tried to break Sebastian out of GenTel. He had even gone undercover as an orderly and tried to offer Sebastian encouragement, reminding him of his name through the locked door to his solitary confinement at Crown Holdings. Cavan had pressed his luck that time, and he was lucky to have survived when he was apprehended. He was even luckier that his coven sister Aine, a powerful witch in her own right, was working her own undercover mission in Numea and could smuggle him back out to the Kingdom.

Sometimes his ribs still ached where the guards on Sebastian's cell had broken them.

None of that mattered now. Sebastian was on his way home, and Cavan was overjoyed. His best friend was safe and healthy, and even though he was currently quite literally in the arms of the enemy, Cavan was certain that the good days were about to return.

At least that's what he told himself.

The sounds of sex died down, and he let out a deep sigh. He hoped that his two charges would just give up and go to sleep now. Azanel would be furious if he heard them, and Cavan couldn't predict what the dragon would do. It was almost enough to make him want to stay on guard all night. He could sleep on the transport. They had another four hours of driving before they reached the walls of Corona, and he was ready for the trip to be over.

One of the guards, the taller of the two lupen, emerged from their room just down the sidewalk. He had a plastic bucket in his hand.

"Hey, man," he said, gesturing with his empty container. "You know where the ice machine is?"

"No idea. Probably down by the office, if they even have one."

"Cool. Thanks."

The lupen walked away and vanished into a side corridor. He returned only moments later, his bucket still empty.

"Good call," he said. "No ice for us."

"These Badlands hotels suck donkey balls."

The guard laughed. He reached his door, then hesitated. "You, uh… you're a witch."

Cavan nodded. "Yeah. Does that bother you?"

"No, not at all. I just don't understand why you helped the Oppressor, that's all. I mean, if you were full human, I might get it, but you're not. You're a mythric like the rest of us."

"What's your name?"

The lupen looked confused by the non sequitur. "Joro."

"Well, Joro, it's like this. The prince was distressed seeing the Oppressor in that condition, and I was worried that he'd have a heart attack if he kept getting low-level electrocuted. Even a demon can only stand that sort of thing for so long."

Joro snorted. "Sick bastard was probably liking it."

"I rather doubt that."

The lupen came closer and joined him in leaning against the wall. Inside the room, the bedsprings began to creak, and Joro raised his eyebrows. "Are you kidding me?"

Cavan laughed quietly. "I wish I was."

"Do you...Should we..."

"I'm not going in there."

"Yeah... me, neither." He scratched at his muzzle. "You're in the Claws, right?"

He nodded. "Yeah. What of it?"

"And the prince was in the Claws."

"Yeah. We were in the same unit."

Joro glanced at the heavily-draped window in the wall Cavan was leaning against. "Do you think that the prince will ever be able to go back?"

That was a question he'd been mulling over, himself. "I guess it depends on how badly they fucked him up."

"Yeah..." A loud moan sounded in the room, and Joro grimaced. "Bad enough, I'd say."

Cavan knew Sebastian's pleasure sounds, and he glowered. "Yeah. Hostage syndrome is in full effect, I think."

"Do you think there's any way to cure him?"

The concern in the lupen's voice was gratifying, and Cavan decided he might start to like this guard. "Maybe, with enough therapy. He has to want to be cured, though. Right now, it sounds like he kind of likes being where he is."

Joro nodded. "Yeah. Clearly." He straightened and gestured with his empty ice bucket again. "Well… have fun."

"Not likely."

Joro smiled and went back into his room, leaving Cavan to listen to the couple in the hotel room.

CHAPTER NINE

CHRISTOPHER

Sebastian was sleeping soundly, overcome by his afterglow, and Christopher lay and watched him quietly. The light in the room was dim, but the serum that had taken his powers could not affect his demonic vision. Hell was a dark place, and seeing in low light was easy for him. He had been born for darkness, after all.

The next morning would bring their arrival in Corona, and he would be delivered to his doom, whatever that might be. A part of him supposed that they might hold him as a hostage to try to force some kind of concession out of the Countess - a plan that would never work - or they might just kill him outright. He hoped that Mythria was not given to ostentatious displays, and that he wouldn't be marched as a prisoner in front of throngs of people. He was chilled by the thought that he might just be given over to those people, many of whom had lost relatives to the Hunters who supplied GenTel with its mythric stock. They would tear him into pieces. He had told the Countess that he would consider it a mercy if she killed him, but dying in such a horrific way was not what he'd had in mind.

He rose from the bed as silently as he could and went to the shower, cleaning away the remaining effects of his torture and the more pleasant experience he and his dragonel had enjoyed that night. Christopher would never have a night like this again, he was certain, and he was grateful to have had it. The memory of this encounter would see him through the dark days ahead.

He felt stronger as the shower continued, and he felt Sebastian's sexual energy seeping at last into his soul, empowering him despite the serum. The more he thought about what the coming day would bring, the more he began to fume. It was madness for him to go placidly into Corona. He had been through too much in his life to just surrender now. If the Mythrians wanted to kill him so badly, and he knew they did, then he would make them work for it.

Yesterday he had been weakened from the alchemical silver, but today he was stronger, and the rest he'd gotten on the bus and tonight in this room had helped him. He assumed that the serum he'd been given that removed or blunted his demonic abilities was similar to the suppressant that he had given the cryptomorphs and to the mythrics in his care. It was powerful, and it weakened them and made them placid. It was also temporary and would always wear off. The drug in his system would no doubt have an end phase as well. The only question was how long it would take to fade. He had never heard of any suppressant for demonic abilities, and in truth, it was surprising to him that anyone knew enough about demons to have made one. The Mythrians and the citizens of Pentepolis were never supposed to even know that there were demons in their midst. He would be interested in finding out how they'd learned.

He shut off the water and toweled dry, his mind made up. He was without demonic powers, but he was a survivor, and he had learned more than a few tricks in his many long years. The Countess and Lord Ashmar had both been his unwitting tutors, and he had learned much both from watching them work and from being on the receiving end of their brutality.

The guard on the door was either the witch or the ice dragon. Ice dragons he knew, and he knew how to incapacitate one. It had been useful information to know when wrangling recalcitrant mythrics in the lab. He knew the pressure point at the base of the neck that would paralyze them temporarily, and he knew which skull plates weren't fused to allow them to shift into their dragon forms. A blow to the right cranial seam could either stun or kill, depending on the power behind the impact. He saw no need to hold back where Azanel was concerned.

The witch was something else. He was physically human, but witchcraft was an in-born wildcard that could not be predicted. He might have been as undefended as a human, or he might have had sorcerous defenses that Christopher could never have imagined. His best bet would be to wait until the guard changed and Azanel took over for the witch before he made his move.

In his entire life, he had only known one witch. Nicholas had been given to him as a gift, a companion meant to fill his days with pleasure, and the young witch had complied. He'd been broken from the wild and trained to perfection before the Countess purchased him, and Nicholas had been Christopher's reward for doing his job well. He'd used his witchcraft for Christopher's ease and luxury. Nicholas had massaged him, created scented oils for their play, healed his injuries when the Countess or Lord Ashmar used him, and soothed his dreams. Nicholas read his palm and tea leaves, and he had embroidered the robe Christopher had worn on his last morning at the Countess's estate. They had been together for many happy years, long enough for the incubus to learn the things that Nicholas enjoyed, what things he disliked, and what things he couldn't bear. They had loved one another in their own way and he still missed him greatly. Witches, like demons, were meant to be immortal. Unfortunately silver blades had a way of ending everything. Nicholas had died at Lord Ashmar's hands, and he'd been forced to watch. Gifts, the Countess told him while he watched Nicholas die, could be taken away.

Christopher pushed the dark memories aside. He dressed and watched Sebastian sleep. He wanted to bring the dragonel along with him, but he didn't know if Sebastian would be open to the idea, and he also didn't know if the dragonel would betray him to the soldiers in the room next door. Christopher had no love for Creek and his ilk, and if he could find a way to destroy them, he would. He still wanted to know what manner of creature this Creek person was, and if he was back in Numea, he would take him for study. The urge to vivisect the creature was almost overpowering. Unfortunately he had to muzzle his scientific curiosity and just concentrate on escaping.

There was a single window in their rented room, and it looked out onto the sidewalk where Cavan was standing. The heavy curtains blocked out light and prevented him from observing his guard's behavior, but he found that if he crouched against the wall at a specific height, he could peer through the miniscule space between curtain and window that was caused by the ledge of the windowsill. It held the curtains out ever so slightly, and if he turned his head just right, he could see the man outside.

Cavan was pacing, his head down. There was something familiar about the man, but perhaps that was just because he was a witch and there was a commonality to the species. Christopher wasn't sure. The other man's steps took him on a repeated path back and forth across the door to their room, and he never strayed more than perhaps a step away from the opening. The door opened into the room, which prevented him from using it as a weapon, but hopefully, if he opened it quietly enough, he would be able to step out without making too much noise or attracting too much attention. From there, he could steal the guards' van and make a break. The transport was too unwieldy to make a good chase vehicle.

Dragons could follow in the air, though, if they were so inclined, and he knew that ice dragons were nimble flyers. His target had to be Azanel.

So Christopher waited for an hour or more, watching Cavan pace. The witch wore a stony expression that never changed. At three in the morning, Azanel came out of his room farther down the sidewalk, and the incubus could hear them talking.

"You're released," Azanel told Cavan.

"They've been quiet for hours. You'll be happy you weren't here a while ago."

Christopher could see the ice dragon's face twist. "I suppose they were… renewing their acquaintance?"

Cavan laughed, and it was a hollow sound. Interesting. "You might say that." He nodded. "I pass the post to you. Good luck staying awake."

"I know my duty, witch."

"Glad to know that can happen once in a while, dragon."

Azanel reached out to grab Cavan's throat, but the witch sidestepped the attempt and batted the dragon's hand away. Azanel hissed, "I will see you burn someday, Waters."

"That'll be hard to do," Cavan told him, amazingly calm for someone who had just been threatened by a presumed ally. "Water doesn't burn."

Azanel sneered at him. "Go away."

Cavan turned and looked at the window, and for a heart-stopping moment, Christopher thought that he had been seen. The witch turned away. "Good luck."

The witch walked down the sidewalk and entered one of the rooms, closing the door behind him. Azanel crossed his arms and leaned against the wall with a disgusted sigh. The side of the door he had chosen was the hinge side, and Christopher could see ways that this position both helped and hurt his plans.

It was nearly go-time. Christopher left his position at the window and picked up the handcuffs that Sebastian had tossed away. He did his best to move them so they didn't clink, and he gripped the cuff parts together so they looped over his knuckles. He considered Sebastian once again, reluctant to leave him. He didn't know what fate awaited him in Corona, but the dragonel was a prince, and he would be well-treated. When that changed, he was clever and strong, and anyway, there was no saying that Christopher or the Countess's Hunters couldn't find him again.

That thought made him uncomfortable, though he couldn't say why. He swallowed the conflicting emotions and left Sebastian with a tender look and a sub-telepathic goodbye.

He crept toward the door and unlocked it, sliding the deadbolt out of the way. It gave the barest of clicks, and he held his breath, waiting for a response. It came not from outside the room, but in the form of a sleepy voice from the bed.

"Christopher?" He looked over at Sebastian, who was sat up in bed, still bleary-eyed. "What are you doing?"

He took a deep breath and answered honestly in a whisper. "I'm leaving."

Sebastian tossed the covers aside and asked softly, "Without me?"

There was hurt in his tone, and it made Christoper wince.

"I'm going back to Numea and I won't take you back to the Countess."

The dragonel approached, running agitated hands through his long blond hair. He kept his voice down, but there was intensity behind his words nonetheless. "But she mistreats you. Why would you go back to her?"

Christopher sighed. "Because it's the only place I belong."

Sebastian was close enough that he could put his hands on his shoulders. "You belong with me."

A jolt of sorrow surprised the incubus, and his eyes stung momentarily before he blinked the new moisture away. "No. You belong in Mythria, and I can't go there."

"But I…" Sebastian trailed off. He spoke again in a hoarse whisper. "I don't belong anywhere."

Impulsively, Christopher embraced him, kissing him deeply. Sebastian kissed him back, and there was desperation in the touch. Christopher realized that he was the only person here that the dragonel knew at all, the only touchstone on his new reality that he had.

Sebastian pulled back. "Let me come with you. We'll find a new place to be. There must be somewhere in the Badlands where we can hide, or somewhere in Mythria…"

He thought hard, then shelved the problem for later consideration. "We'll figure it out once we get out of here."

Sebastian glanced at the door. "Is there a guard?"

Christopher nodded. "Azanel."

The dragonel's golden eyes flickered down to the handcuffs in the demon's fist. He nodded. "I'll call him in. You take him out."

They kissed once more, then Christopher took cover behind the door. Sebastian hurriedly cleaned up, dressed, and sat down on the bed. When they were both ready, the dragonel raised his voice.

"Azanel!"

The door opened immediately, and the ice dragon stepped inside. Sebastian rose and hurried toward him, and Azanel took a step toward the dragonel.

"Seb -"

Christopher brought his improvised brass knuckles down hard on the crown of Azanel's head, splitting the skin. The dragon fell like a sack of bricks, pale pink blood staining his hair. Sebastian stepped over his prone body and looked out.

The guards' door opened, and the two lupen emerged, weapons in their hands. Sebastian charged at them, and they held their fire in confusion. He grabbed a pistol from one and shoved him back into the hotel room. Christopher hurried to join him, and he ripped the weapon away from the second lupen guard. A bullet to the head stopped his resistance forever.

Creek lurched up from the bed as Sebastian threw Joro onto Clayven. Christopher gunned the reptilian down and grabbed the van keys from the top of the dresser.

"Let's go."

As Joro and Clayven wrestled out of one another's way and out of the room, Christopher and Sebastian sprinted for the van. A bullet whistled past them, and the demon looked back to see Kliyo with a rifle in her hands. Cavan grabbed the weapon and pushed it skyward, his voice carrying across the parking lot.

"Stop! You'll shoot the prince!"

They reached the van and threw themselves into the front seats, Christopher taking the wheel. Sebastian held on while the demon floored the accelerator, peeling out of the parking lot as fast as the van could go.

"We need to ditch this beast for something faster," Sebastian said. "We're never going to get away in this."

"They only have the transport," Christopher disagreed. "That'll never go fast enough."

"Azanel can fly."

"Not today, he can't." He risked a grin. "We did it."

The smile Sebastian gave him in return was uncertain, and he looked down at the pistol he still held. "We'll need more ammunition, and more gas for the van, as well as a map."

Christopher chuckled, exhilarated by their escape. "We also need a clue, but we can get all of that in Kristal."

"Are there other settlements?"

"A few nomad camps, some little hard-scrabble towns," Christopher answered. "Kristal is big and lawless, and we can easily lose ourselves there while we look for what we need."

Sebastian took a deep breath, and when he spoke, his words came out almost like a warning. "I'm trusting you."

"I know." Christopher took his eyes off the road long enough to look at Sebastian. "I won't disappoint you."

CHAPTER TEN

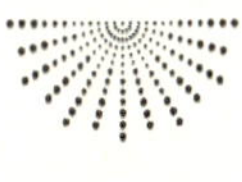

CAVAN

Cavan took the rifle from Kliyo as Joro and Clayven emerged from their room, their weapons in their hands. They stopped when they saw their fellow guard lying dead on the sidewalk.

"He shot Creek," Joro announced to the witch.

"Who did?"

"The Oppressor."

He nodded, his lips pressed into a thin line. He went into the room where Sebsatian and Christopher had been staying, followed closely by the others. He stopped short when he saw the ice dragon's inert body lying on the floor. Cavan bent over Azanel, studying the injury to his head. "He needs medical attention. We need to get him to Mythria as soon as possible."

Beside him, Kliyo was in a panic. "But the prince…"

"I will find him. Take the two surviving guards and get Prince Azanel to the hospital in Zyros. It's just over the border, and they can help him there." He stood and wiped the ice dragon's pale blood from his hands onto the bedspread. "I'll go after the prince."

Kliyo's voices were harsh. "Kill the Oppressor if you have to."

"Gladly."

The prince's assistant gathered up the guards and set about obeying the orders Cavan had given her. He looked around the room briefly, checking the rumpled sheets for signs of blood or scales, wanting to prove to himself that Sebastian was physically unhurt. When he was satisfied, he went to the office manager's room, rifle in hand.

The half-satyr opened the door warily. He had to have heard the gunshots and was afraid, as any reasonable civilian would be. He looked at Cavan.

"Is it safe?"

"Yes. I need a vehicle. A fast one."

"I don't have a vehicle."

Cavan was annoyed. "How do you get supplies for the hotel, then?"

The man licked his lips nervously. "I… they're brought to me. Every morning, a new shipment comes in. Listen, vehicles and gasoline are hard to come by out here in the Badlands. The Kingdom and Pentepolis don't have to worry about that, but we do. I can't afford a car."

"You must have something in case of emergencies."

"Well…" He hesitated, and Cavan could see the calculations in the man's brain.

With a disgusted sigh, he took a credit chip out of his pocket. "I'll give you the password and everything loaded on this is yours if you have something worth trading for it."

The hotel owner's eyes lit up, and he looked at the chip in excitement. "I have a motorcycle."

"Tank full?"

He nodded. "Yes."

The hotel manager reached for the chip, but Cavan pulled it away. "Keys first."

He watched as the other man hurried to pull the keys out of a desk drawer. They were on a keyring attached to a green plastic dragon. "It's parked behind the tool shed."

Cavan took the dragon off the ring and handed it back along with the chip. The manager immediately put the chip into his reader. "The passcode is 2176. Don't spend it all in one place."

He took the keys and hurried out to the tool shed. The motorcycle was parked where the manager said it would be, and it looked like it had been kept together with chewing gum and baling wire. Cavan knew he would never catch up with the van using such a dilapidated machine, but at least he could follow their trail.

He started the engine with some difficulty, then drove at the highest speed he could manage out onto the road. The dry conditions of the Badlands meant that the dust cloud created by the van's passing was still hanging in the air, and he could see the vehicle far ahead. As long as he could keep the dust cloud in sight, he could follow the trail.

Cavan wasn't certain what he was going to do when he caught up with them. He was certain that he would be no match for a dragonel and a demon if they were determined to fight, and anyway, he had no interest in coming to blows with them. He wouldn't force Sebastian to go back to Corona. The dragonel had already been forced too many times and in too many ways.

He had things he needed to tell Sebastian, and now that Azanel was nowhere near, he was free to say them. He knew the dragonel, and had known him for years; if anyone would be able to help him recover the lost pieces of himself, it was Cavan. He was less enthusiastic about Christopher hearing their conversation, but Sebastian had become attached to the incubus for reasons that eluded Cavan. The dragonel had left voluntarily. There would be no separating the two fugitives.

The van turned, taking the road to Kristal. It was the only destination that made any sense. The city was more than a day away, so he knew that Sebastian and Christopher would have to stop. He would catch up with them then.

Another dust cloud appeared on the horizon, heralding the arrival of a quintet of motorcycles tearing toward him at high speed. He ran a hand over his eyes and whispered a word of power, and he gained the ability to see as if he were looking through a telescope. The bikes the newcomers rode were in much better condition than the one he had, and they showed customizations that made them even faster. The lead rider had lupen tails attached to the handlebars, and that was all Cavan needed to see to know who they were.

Hunters.

He was not going to let the Hunters catch up with Sebastian. They would be only too happy to drag him back to Numea. He would not allow that to happen.

He had no love for Hunters. They had raided the little village where he'd been born, and his mother and brother had been carried off, never to be seen again. There had at one time been a high premium paid by the Community for witch companions, and of the three of them, he was the least powerful. He was fortunate that he was a scrappy child and made the Hunters work too hard; they'd let him go when it was clear he would be more of a handful than they wanted to deal with. His mother and Nicholas, though, hadn't been as lucky, and to this day, he cursed himself for spending his energy on saving himself instead of helping them.

The motorcycle he was riding coughed and sputtered beneath him, and he knew he would never reach his dragonel in time. The Hunters were closer, and their bikes were faster. He only hoped that somehow Sebastian and Christopher could hold off the onslaught until he could arrive and back them up.

∾

CHRISTOPHER

THE VAN WAS unwieldy and hardly a fast getaway vehicle, but it was serviceable and certainly was faster than the transport. Christopher saw a cloud of dust rising from the road behind them, as well as the smaller cloud from a pursuing motorcycle. He guessed that the one driving the bike was either the witch or one of the surviving guards. His money was on the witch.

The dragonel in the passenger seat was watching the same motorcycle in the side view mirror, his hands on his knees.

"Don't worry," Christopher told him. "I don't think he can catch up with us."

"What do you think he'd do if he did?" Sebastian asked.

The incubus shrugged. "Shoot me and drag you back, probably."

Sebastian turned and looked at him with his extraordinary golden eyes. "I don't want that, on either count."

He smiled. "Neither do I."

The dragonel chuckled. "I would imagine you'd really like to avoid the getting shot part."

"Actually," Christopher admitted, "the part that would bother me the most would be losing you to them again."

A slow, warm smile spread across Sebastian's face. It was one of the loveliest smiles Christopher had ever seen. "Well, don't worry. You're not going to lose me."

"I hope not." He turned back to face the road ahead and confessed, "That would break my heart."

Sebastian looked closely at him, his eyes slightly narrowed as he searched Christopher's face. The moment of scrutiny passed, and then the dragonel raised an eyebrow. "You have a heart?"

The playful tone in Sebastian's voice filled Christopher with happiness. Sebastian had never joked with him before. "Yes," he admitted, grinning and overjoyed that they had reached a new level of comfort. "It's small and withered and I keep it in the medicine cabinet."

"Appropriate for a doctor."

The incubus was grateful that Sebastian hadn't used the more fraught term 'veterinarian.' He hoped that meant that the dragonel was beginning to see past the trappings of what he'd done and what he'd been forced to do while in the Countess's clutches.

Sebastian looked back at the motorcycle. "He's not going very fast. It's almost like he doesn't want to catch us."

"That machine is a piece of shit. He'll never catch up."

"Good."

Another cloud of dust, this one ahead of them, caught his attention. Christopher frowned as he made out a set of speedier motorcycles bearing down on them. Grumbling, he turned the van onto a side road, heading directly to Kristal instead of toward the distant northern lake he'd wanted to reach.

"Sebastian," he said, keeping his voice as casual as he could, "do you remember how to fight?"

The dragonel looked at him almost warily. "Fight how?"

"Since we don't have weapons, mostly tooth and nail."

Sebastian turned and looked out the window at the motorcycles. "Who is that?"

"Hunters." He glanced at them in the rear-view. "I think I might actually know them."

"Is that a good thing or a bad thing?"

"Very, very bad." He pushed the accelerator harder, and the van shook as it increased speed to its highest level. "They're not the sort of people I ever wanted to see again, and I really don't want you to encounter them."

"They'd take me back to Crown Holdings," Sebastian said, sounding quesy.

"Or worse. They also sell to the gladiator school in Kristal." He glanced at the dragonel. "You're a pretty substantial hunk of meat, especially with those shoulders, and they'd love to make a killer out of you."

He looked seriously at Christopher and asked in a grave voice, "If I was one of the King's Talons, then I was already a killer."

The demon couldn't tell if that thought was horrifying or reassuring to Sebastian, or if it carried unwelcome memories. He supposed that at this point, any memory at all would be a blessing as far as the dragonel was concerned. The neural editing had stolen so much from him. He wondered if anything he'd heard the Kingdom forces telling Sebastian had been true, and how much had been invented to take advantage of the dragonel's tortured mind.

"I know they said you were a fighter," Christopher reassured him. "But I'm sure it's not like you were an assassin or some sort of murderer in a uniform."

He could hear the motorcycle engines now, announcing that the squad of Hunters was gaining ground. "Look in the back and see if there are any weapons."

Sebastian left his seat and made his way into the cargo area of the van. Christopher could see him searching under the seats and in a gear crate that was strapped down near the back doors. The dragonel pulled out a rifle and automatically checked the charges and flipped the safety off. It seemed that some memories were coming back to him, after all.

"Try to keep the van steady," Sebastian told him, settling into position with the rifle like a sniper.

"Do you know how to shoot?" Christopher asked.

"I was a Talon," he answered firmly, "and even if I was away for a year, I'm pretty sure some things became reflexive."

"Like marksmanship?" the incubus asked doubtfully.

Sebastian readied the rifle. "I guess we'll find out."

SEBASTIAN

AS SOON AS Sebastian held the rifle in his hands, a feeling of familiarity washed over him. For the first time in his remaining memory, he felt like he was doing something he had done a hundred times before. He had doubted Azanel and the others when they told him that he'd been a soldier, but now he was absolutely certain they'd been telling him the truth. The rifle in his hands, the smell of the oil, and the feeling of sighting down the barrel at a moving target made him feel at home for the first time since he'd woken up suspended from the Crown Holdings ceiling. Here at last was something he knew he could do.

Sebastian watched as the motorcycles approached the van. The man on the front bike raised his fist to signal his fellows, and he realized that the bikes all had weapons mounted to the steering columns, aiming down the front tire. They sped toward them in a wedge formation, and the man in the center had the biggest gun.

"They're armed," he told Christopher.

The demon began to swerve back and forth as he drove,

which was not at all holding steady the way Sebastian had asked him to do. It was evasive, though, and any bullets the Hunters fired would be more likely to miss. He felt the weight of the rifle in his hands and knew that he could compensate.

The two Hunters flanking the lead bike opened fire, one shooting wide, one shooting low. Sebastian aimed and made no such mistake. With lethal accuracy, he sent one bullet through the face of man on the lead bike. He dropped dead instantly, his head dissolving into a pink mist. His bike flipped onto its side while his corpse went sprawling, and between the body and the bike, the next two riders in the formation lost control and skidded off the roadway, crashing into the rocky ground.

"Three left," he announced to Christopher.

The demon replied in a tone that left no room for argument. "Make it zero."

Sebastian bent and took aim again, but before he could pull the trigger, a shot from the motorcycle that had pursued them from the motel dropped one of the riders. He was impressed that the gunman had been able to make such a deadly shot from such a distance, but he shelved his admiration for later. He still had work to do. Sebastian squeezed the trigger and shot. His bullet ripped into the chest of one of the men, and a slug from the pursuer hit the last Hunter between the shoulder blades and sent him slumping over his handlebars.

WIth no riders to control them, the motorcycles careened out of control, and a pile of broken and twisted debris blocked the road.Sebastian nodded to himself, satisfied with a job well done, and a distant memory of a drill sergeant screaming in his ear played in his mind. The sergeant had been a bear shifter, and he still remembered the creature's hot breath on the back of his neck. His hair must have been shorter then.

Sebastian shook the memory away and looked at the lone rider who still remained. He raised the rifle and took careful aim, but when he looked through the sight, he hesitated. It was Cavan, and he found it difficult to pull the trigger. He could have killed him, and if he fired now, with his sights set on the witch's heart, he could have ended his pursuit, but the thought of doing so filled him with something very much like nausea. He aimed at the tire instead, blowing it out with a single shot. Cavan's motorcycle flipped forward and sent its rider flying into the sandy ground. Sebastian felt sick, wondering what injuries the witch had suffered, not wanting to leave him dead or dying out in the desert. The van kept speeding away, though, and he watched Cavan's inert form lying in the gravel beside the road until he could see him no longer.

He was confused. One minute he felt strong and power-ful, tapping into half-remembered military memories, and the next minute he was a pacifist again. He didn't know which was the real Sebastian.

He didn't know if he'd ever find out for sure.

THEY DROVE until they reached another dumpy hotel. This one was in even sadder shape than the ones they'd already stayed in, with some of the windows broken out and the parking lot rutted and full of potholes. The paint had been scoured off the big sign that stood on two tall poles, and the name of the place was obscured. Only the neon "open" sign in the office window gave any indication that the place was occupied.

"Nice place," Sebastian commented, leaning forward and looking through the windshield. Christopher snorted.

On the horizon, a heavy cloud was gathering, obscuring the low-slanting light of the evening sun. Instead of grey or white, though, this cloud was brown. They both saw it gathering at the same time.

"What is that?" the dragonel asked.

"Sandstorm." Christopher shook his head. "There are a lot of them out here in the north of the Badlands."

Without obtaining permission from the proprietor, he parked the van on the sidewalk of the breezeway that connected the office to the hotel proper. Sebastian looked at him quizzically.

"This should keep the van as protected as possible from the sandstorm, and hopefully there won't be any damage to the engine," the demon explained.

"Well, here's hoping."

They had no luggage. Sebastian found a set of bungee cords and several padlocks, and he tied and locked the gun case shut. Even so, he brought the rifle and several extra clips with him, just in case. Christopher watched him working with an intense stare, and he carried the rest of the cords, hooks and locks into the hotel office when they went in.

There was a wobbly desk made of pressboard and wood veneer just inside the door, and a man sitting on a cracked plastic chair. He was more than half drunk, a mostly-empty bottle of something alcoholic and likely homemade dangling from his hand. When he saw Sebastian and Christopher, his eyes widened, and he stared at the rifle in the dragonel's hand.

"I don't want no trouble," he said, nearly weeping with fright, "and I don't have no money."

"I don't want your money," Christopher said coldly. "I want your best room."

The man reached into a desk and pulled out a metal key with a diamond-shaped plastic tag. He practically threw it at the demon. "Here. Room three. Best in the house."

"Do you have electricity and running water in the room?"

The man nodded. "Yes."

"Food and drink?"

He scrunched up his face. "Vending machine." He looked at Sebastian's rifle again. "If you hit it on the side, it'll give you whatever you want. You don't have to pay."

"Excellent." Christopher picked up the key. "If you come anywhere near us tonight, my friend here will blow your head off. Understand?"

The man nodded again, terror in his eyes. "You, uh… You're the Oppressor. Aren't you?"

Sebastian looked at Christopher, waiting for his response. He wasn't sure how this clerk knew who his companion was, and for the first time, he wondered about who had chosen the name the people in the Kingdom and the Badlands called him. The demon smiled, and it was a look so like the ones that the Countess gave that it made Sebastian's blood run cold.

"I am. If you know that, then you must know what I'm capable of, and what will happen to you if you disturb or betray us."

There was ice and steel in Christopher's tone, and it reminded Sebastian of Lord Ashmar. The mental image of the demon bound to the Countess's stocks and being beaten by Lord Ashmar rose in his mind, and to his dismay, he found his cock hardening at the thought. Christopher glanced at him, and his dark eyes seemed darker than before. Sebastian wasn't certain if that was a trick of the light, darkened as it was by the approaching sandstorm, or if the serum suppressing his demonic abilities was starting to wear off. He was almost afraid to ask.

The clerk began to weep in his terror. "I... I know. I won't say a word to anybody. I swear."

"Good." That almost soulless smile returned to Christopher's face. "I'd hate to repay your hospitality with pain. Come along, dragonel."

Sebastian followed him obediently. For a moment, he almost felt the collar around his neck again.

CHAPTER ELEVEN

SEBASTIAN

*C*hristopher led him across the breezeway and into the body of the hotel. There was a small, shabby lobby equipped with a billiards table and a bar that was devoid of alcohol. The clerk had probably drunk all of it, judging from the empty bottle haphazardly strewn around the floor.

"Can't say I think much of the housekeepers," Sebastian said.

Christopher looked at him with a smirk but said nothing.The dragonel fell silent.

They went through a double door and found their room at the end of a short hallway, across from an alcove holding a clearly defunct ice machine and a battered snack box that was half filled with candy that was probably stale. Sebastian had no intention of eating anything there.

The key slid easily into the lock and clicked, and the door swung open. The room was small, but it had a queen-sized brass bed that looked welcoming enough. There was a scuffed dresser and a small cafe table, but no chairs. There was a single window that was open to the outside world, and he could see the storm coming closer. The wind was picking up, and it was starting to whistle around the window, whose seal left a great deal to be desired. The demon pulled the curtain shut, blocking out the light and the sand.

"Best room," Christopher snorted softly. "If this is his best, I'd hate to see his worst." He went into the en suite bathroom and looked around while Sebastian watched him through the open doorway. The demon picked up a tiny plastic bottle and opened it, sniffing at the contents. The scent, which to Sebastian was a chemical version of vanilla, apparently passed muster, because he simply recapped the bottle. "At least it has toiletries."

The place couldn't hold a candle to the Countess's house in Numea, or even to the farmhouse they had fled to just before they'd been captured by Azanel and his men. Sebastian shrugged.

"It's better than a prison cell."

Christopher put the bungee straps, carabiners and locks down on the table beside the little plastic bottle and sat on the bed. "How long were you in solitary at Crown Holdings?"

Sebastian didn't want to think back to those days, but he also didn't want to ignore the demon's question. He didn't want to disobey, and he wondered why he had that impulse again. Maybe it was because they were alone, or because he was in a position again where he was mystified and depending on Christopher, who seemed like the only person who knew what was going on. He couldn't say.

"A few weeks, maybe? Several days? I don't know. It all ran together."

He put the rifle and ammunition on the dresser and sat beside Christopher, who took his hand. His thumb gently rubbed the tiny scales on Sebastian's skin. "Were you treated horribly?"

"I don't know why you're asking. Weren't you there?"

"At Crown Holdings? Yes, but I wasn't involved in your care."

His *care*. Sebastian frowned at the gentle euphemism for captivity. "You said you catalogued the samples."

"Well… I did that. It was part of what I did in the lab."

He felt a pang of sorrow and asked, "And did you impregnate females with my *samples*?"

Christopher looked at him. "A few."

Sebastian let out a disgusted exhalation and stood up. He started to stalk toward the door, but Christopher snapped at him.

"Stop!"

Against all reason, he did. He turned to face the incubus warily. Christopher was on his feet, too, and the look on his face was so commanding and powerful that Sebastian's knees felt weak. He didn't understand the things that he was feeling.

"Come back here."

He should have walked. He still had the rifle, and he should have shot Christopher and taken his chances in the storm. He should have gone out and tried to make a life for himself away from everyone who claimed to know him. The thought should have been empowering, but instead it filled him with apprehension. He had no idea where to go, or how to handle the things he might find. He had no memory of the Badlands or anywhere else, and he didn't know how to make his way in the world with his head so disconnected.

He obeyed.

Christopher nodded, satisfied, and put his hand on Sebastian's neck, his fingers brushing the dragonel's hair and his thumb stroking the softness of his ear lobe. The touch was intimate and sweet, and Sebastian turned his face into it, thinking how strange it was to see Christopher without gloves. He kissed the demon's scarred palm, and an answering tingle danced along his lips.

"Your powers are coming back," he dared to say.

"Yes, they are."

The simple acknowledgement was thrilling and terrifying at once. Those powers had allowed Christopher to take control of Sebastian's mind back in Numea, and he had compelled him to do things against his will. He was afraid of what Christopher might do to him now, but deep inside, a kernel of his soul was thrilled with the chance to be in his control again. Hesitantly, he met Christopher's gaze. Those expressive brown eyes had gone completely black, and his spirit was caught in the power of the incubus.

"If you obey me voluntarily, I won't force you," the demon said, his voice a husky whisper. "You told me once that you accepted me as your Master. Is that still true?"

He closed his eyes before he answered, wanting to be certain that the words were really his. "Yes."

"Then strip and get on your knees."

Sebastian obeyed again. He took off the uniform he was wearing and put it aside, folding it neatly out of habit formed from kinetic memory. While he was occupied, Christopher busied himself selecting bindings from the cords on the table. Sebastian's heart pounded in fear and dizzy anticipation as he knelt on the filthy carpet. His erection was rampant already, and instead of hiding it with his hands according to his first instinct, he adopted the position he had been trained to take for the Countess's dinner party. He spread his knees and locked his arms behind his back, his hands holding the opposite elbows, his chest and hips pushed out.

Christopher turned and looked at him, and he smiled. "Very good. You remembered."

"Yes, sir."

He had bungee cords in his hands, as well as carabiners and hooks to connect them. He walked around behind Sebastian and bound his right wrist to his right ankle. He used another cord to bind his left wrist and ankle together. He locked the cords into place and came around to stand in front of Sebastian.

"Do you trust me, Sebastian?"

He looked up into Christopher's face. His eyes had gone back to brown again, but he knew that his demonic power was still alive and ready to be put to use. He feared him, and he wanted him, and he searched his heart for the answer to Christopher's question.

"Yes, sir."

He smiled warmly. "Good. Please know that I will never hurt you. I might cause you pain, but I will never hurt you. Do you understand the difference?"

He contemplated his words, then nodded. There would be pain, but not serious injury. Part of him dreaded it, but part of him craved it. "Yes, sir."

"Do you agree to put yourself into my hands, to do whatever I tell you to do, and to endure whatever I choose to do to you?"

The question made him shiver, but not entirely in a bad way. He felt conflicted and confused, but he burned for the man before him. He felt his pulse speed up. "Yes, sir."

"If it ever gets to be too much and you need a moment, say 'mercy.' Do you understand?"

"Yes, sir."

"And if you need me to stop, if it's all too much to bear, say 'red.' Do you understand?"

Sebastian swallowed. He could not imagine Christopher doing anything to him that he would be unable to withstand, but the fact that it was being mentioned meant it was a possibility, and that there might have been something truly painful that the incubus had planned. He was afraid.

"Yes, sir."

Christopher nodded. "Excellent."

He disrobed, putting his oversized, borrowed clothes aside. As he revealed himself, Sebastian thought that his Master's body was the most beautiful he had ever seen. He watched him closely. When Christopher turned to face him once again, he trailed his gaze from the incubus's bare feet and well-toned legs to the heavy cock that jutted out from his hips, the head darker than the shaft, tempting him.

"Sir," he began. "May I…"

"You don't make requests. You follow orders. Am I clear?"

He stifled a sigh. "Yes, sir."

Christopher grasped his chin tightly and made him look into his face. "I want you to suck me until I cum."

Sebastian thought it was no accident that he'd just been ordered to do the very thing he'd tried to ask for. He nodded and ran his tongue over his bottom lip. Christopher chuckled.

"You are such an eager little slut," he praised.

He saw no reason to deny it. "Yes, sir. Only for you, sir."

The demon held his cock steady and rubbed the head against Sebastian's lips. The dragonel licked away the tiny smear of salty moisture that he left behind, and the taste was like ambrosia. He loved Christopher's pre-cum. He looked up at his Master through his golden eyelashes, and the demon let him take him in his mouth, but slowly, an inch at a time. His cock filled Sebastian's mouth, then gradually nudged its way down his throat, and he swallowed around it, trying to take it all and give his Master pleasure. Christopher groaned, and Sebastian was delighted. He pulled back, sliding the hot flesh from his throat but not releasing it from his lips. As slowly as before, he took him in again.

"Oh, yes," Christopher moaned. His mental voice spoke in Sebastian's head, but it sounded a million miles away. His powers were back, but not yet at full strength, it seemed. - *You are a treasure.*-

Sebastian closed his eyes and bobbed his head in a lazy rhythm, dragging Christopher's pleasure out for as long as he could. When he could bear it no longer, the demon clutched the dragonel's hair and held his head steady so he could fuck his mouth. His dick head rammed the back of Sebastian's throat, gagging him, but the dragonel held on, too delighted by the feeling to pull away. Christopher reached his zenith with a cry, and Sebastian swallowed every drop, savoring the taste.

The incubus stepped back rubbing his erection. He didn't go soft after only one round unlike humans, and Sebastian wondered exactly how many times he could go before his body just couldn't function anymore. He hoped that he'd have the time to find out.

Christopher stroked himself a few times, his flushed cheeks and wet, shining eyes making his face a mask of orgasmic aftershocks. Sebastian sat back on his heels and waited, his own cock desperate for attention.

His Master picked Sebastian up, no mean feat considering how muscular and heavy the dragonel was, and put him on the bed. With his arms and feet connected, he lay with his cheek pressed into the bedspread and his ass in the air, presented to Christopher to do with as he pleased. The utter helplessness of the position he'd found himself in made him feel ashamed, but it also made his cock get even harder until it was almost painful, straining for release.

"Pain and pleasure are uniquely connected," Christopher told him, his voice a low, sexy growl. "In the right mindset, they're difficult to distinguish or to separate from one another."

He rested his hand on Sebastian's hip, then slid it down over his buttock, gently squeezing the firm globe. With a crack, he slapped him, and Sebastian jolted, surprised. His flesh tingled and and stung, and he was sure that Christopher had left a handprint. He hoped that he had. He wanted to be marked by him, to be able to show the world proof that he was voluntarily owned by this gorgeous man. There was another sharp slap, and then his other cheek matched the first, another handprint smarting on his skin.

Christopher reached his left hand between Sebastian's legs and trailed his fingers over his taint, gently teasing the sensitive area with feather-light touches, all the while delivering more punishing slaps to his buttocks. Each blow made his ass cheeks vibrate, and the sensations went straight to his cock. Christopher's hand began to stroke him, his grip firm but not punishing, while the spanking continued.

The demon abruptly released him and ran his palm, slick with Sebastian's pre-cum, over the hot skin of his paddled rump. The dragonel moaned in pain and pleasure, and his Master bent to kiss the small of his back.

"Good boy," he praised.

Sebastian felt Christopher kneeling on the mattress behind him, and he expected to be fucked, but instead he felt the incubus's mouth closing over his hole. Christopher's tongue lapped at him, teasing the sensitive pucker while Sebastian gasped. He pushed back against his mouth, encouraging him, and Christopher gripped his hips to hold him still. He continued to lick and suck, enticing the sphincter to open for him until Sebastian's body was begging him for something more than just his tongue.

His Master straightened and retrieved the plastic bottle he'd taken from the bathroom. He opened the top and Sebastian could smell hand lotion. Christopher upended the bottle over the cleft in the dragonel's buttocks and squeezed, letting the cool, slick liquid drip down onto his heated flesh. It ran down over his hole, greasing him.

"Can't have you hurt, now can we? We both know that your spit wasn't quite enough last night."

"It was... enough..."

"Don't argue with me."

The tone was mild even if the words were not, and Sebastian fell silent. He felt Christopher's dick head rubbing against his pucker, and he pushed back. His Master stopped his motion.

"Not yet. Patience."

Sebastian whimpered, which made Christopher chuckle. He rubbed against him again, then pushed inside, taking him an inch at a time. The dragonel moaned. Slowly, inexorably, Christopher sank into him until he was completely sheathed inside Sebastian's body. He draped himself over the dragonel's back and kissed the valley between his shoulder blades, his lips toying with the scales there. He wrapped his arms around Sebastian's waist and held him tight.

"You feel so good," his Master breathed, and then he started to move.

It was pure delight. He was filled to capacity, and his pleasure spot was being rubbed just right as Christopher fucked him. He squeezed his eyes shut and stroked his Master's legs with his bound hands, feeling the muscles flexing with each thrust.

He had been close before, and now it was almost more than he could bear. He panted out, "Master, may I cum?"

"Not yet."

He groaned. "I don't know if I can wait..."

"You'd fucking better," Christopher warned, "or there'll be hell to pay."

The irony of a demon threatening him with hell made Sebastian laugh breathily, which was possibly the wrong thing to do at that moment. Christopher grabbed a handful of his hair and yanked his head back.

"Something funny to you, boy?"

"No, sir."

The hand in his hair twisted his head slightly, just enough to allow his Master to steal a kiss. He moaned against Christopher's lips, and his Master took the hint, speeding up the pace as he drove into his body. He held Sebastian's head up while his other hand gripped his hip, and his thrusts came harder and faster.

"Sir…."

His heated groan made Christopher's cock twitch deep within him, and the incubus said, "You can cum now."

The words added to the sensations he was feeling and drove him over the edge. He wailed as he came, spurting onto the bedspread and spasming around Christopher. The incubus let out a breathy cry and came, pumping into him. He collapsed onto Sebastian's back as he spent the last of his seed inside the dragonel.

When it was over, Christopher gently untied him, and they got under the soiled covers. The incubus took Sebastian in his arms and held him close, stroking his face lovingly. With his head on his Master's shoulder, the dragonel slid off into easy, dreamless sleep.

CHAPTER TWELVE

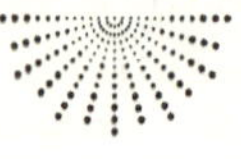

CAVAN

$\mathcal{H}$e woke to darkness, and it took him a moment to realize that it was because night had fallen, not because he was dead. He had to admit that the shot to his tire had been a good one, and he appreciated that Sebastian hadn't shot him in the face the way he had the lead Hunter. He would have appreciated it more if the dragonel hadn't nearly blasted him into the afterworld.

He groaned and rolled onto his side. When he'd gone flying over the handlebars of the motorcycle, he'd flipped completely, his heels hitting the ground first before his butt, followed quickly by his back and his head. He was one big bruise, and from the agony in his feet, he was certain his heels were broken. He put his hand to the back of his head, and it came away bloody. He groaned again, pained and annoyed.

He didn't know what else he'd expected. Of course Sebastian would default back to his Numean programming as soon as he was alone with the Oppressor. It was what he'd been trained to do, probably at great length and with massive suffering. He didn't blame him. He understood why he was running with Christopher, and why he was defending him.

Understanding didn't mean he wasn't angry about it, though.

He was covered in sand, and his head injury had kept him from noticing that his exposed skin was bloody and rough from being scoured by the sandstorm. He was grateful in a way that he hadn't been awake for his sandpaper bath, but on the other hand, if he'd been conscious, he might have been able to protect himself. Too late now.

He heard gravel shifting and looked back to see one of the Hunters picking himself up off the ground. He was the one who had fired on the van first, one of the two who'd flanked the lead Hunter. He hadn't been shot; instead, he'd been fouled up when his bike ran over the nearly headless corpse of his leader and wiped out on the road. The Hunter was bloody from road rash and staggering, disoriented, but unlike his fellows he'd been wearing a helmet, which had probably saved him from a killing head wound. As it was, he likely had a concussion.

Cavan hadn't been wearing a helmet, and his own road rash was considerable. He was in bad shape and he knew it. He'd been using the rifle he'd taken from Kliyo, and he had impressed himself with his own ability to shoot the two Hunters he'd killed. No minor accomplishment, really, firing a rifle one-handed while going high speed on a shuddering bike that threatened to come unglued beneath him. The fact that he had used his magic to steady the rifle did nothing to take away from his feat.

That's what he was going to tell himself, anyway, so he could congratulate himself on being a stud while he died in the dirt.

The sole surviving Hunter shuffled forward and poked at the nearest body. He grunted when he saw the death wound in the other Hunter's back. Cavan lay still, hoping that the disoriented man hadn't seen him, knowing he was in no condition to fight. His rifle lay in the dirt several yards away, far out of reach. His only hope was to play dead and hope that the Hunter believed he was dead.

The Hunter dragged himself forward, one leg not quite fully functional but still in use. Cavan had to respect the man's determination. He had always been one to give his enemies at least grudging respect, and this was no different. Any adversary worth fighting had qualities to be admired, he had been taught.

He nearly laughed at himself. He couldn't make himself focus on the very real danger this Hunter posed, too busy letting his mind wander along philosophical paths. He was going to get himself killed if he didn't pay attention. Wool-gathering, his grandmother had called it. A line from an old nursery rhyme played through his head, and against all reason, he whispered it out loud, all the while wondering why he was daft enough to do so.

"Yes, sir, yes, sir, three bags full."

The Hunter turned toward him when he whispered, and Cavan's delirium made the other man's startled expression the funniest thing he'd ever seen. He grinned, too weak to laugh, and held out his hand toward his rifle. A word of power twitched inside his brain, but he couldn't make his tongue pronounce it.

"You still alive, boy?" the Hunter grunted.

"Seems like."

The Hunter fumbled with a pistol, trying with a complete lack of coordination to drag it from its holster. Cavan's power word finally found its way from his brain to his tongue, and he spoke it aloud. The rifle flew from its sandy resting spot to his hand.

"Fuck. Witch!" the Hunter exclaimed. "No way! Witches is only females."

"Guess again."

He pointed the rifle at the Hunter and fired. His body hit the ground with a thud, and Cavan dropped his hand and head into the dirt again. This time, he held onto the rifle.

He lost consciousness again, and when he opened his eyes again, the sky was steel-grey with the coming dawn. His head felt clearer, which on one hand was good because it gave him the ability to try to help himself; on the other hand, it was bad because his pain was that much more noticeable now that he wasn't dazed. Pain hovered around him like a red cloud, and he knew he had to do something before he could get back on the road and find Sebastian.

He thought maybe he should go back, but at this point, he was in the middle of nowhere, as far from home as he was from the dragonel. He had to get Sebastian away from Christopher, and the thought of what the Oppressor might be doing to the dragonel gave him a surge of anger that came with enough energy to sit up.

Cavan dragged himself up to his feet, using his rifle as a crutch, careful to keep the muzzle pointed away from his face. It would have been almost fitting if he blew his own head off in his ineptitude. He was annoyed with himself for his helplessness, and with his injuries. He needed to get to Sebastian. He didn't have time for this.

He managed to make his way to the nearest bike, and to his delight, one of the mirrors had survived the crash. He pulled it free and sat down heavily with the mirror in his hands. He passed his hand through the air above the glass and whispered more words of magic. The image in the mirror shifted, no longer showing his abraded face. Instead, it showed the road ahead, flying over it like a plane, following the only highway to a turn off. The image blinked out as soon as the scrying sensor took the turn, and he sighed. His energy was low.

Cavan had used almost all of his energy on these few parlor tricks, and there was almost nothing left for him to try to heal himself. He was in terrible trouble, and he knew it. Fixing his mind on Sebastian and doing his damnedest to ignore the pain in his feet, he forced himself to start walking.

The road was covered in a heavy layer of fine sand, which made his staggering harder to do. His broken heels were agonizing, but he pushed himself onward, keeping his mind on Sebastian and his need to save the dragonel from himself. Cavan nearly faltered several times, and only his dedication to the Crown Prince kept him going.

He heard the sound of an approaching engine, and he left the road, taking cover behind a patch of scrubby bushes and readying his rifle. He only had a few shots left, and he intended to make them count. If more Hunters were coming, he'd have to choose his targets wisely.

The vehicle that approached was not a Hunter motorcycle gang, and it wasn't a target. It was Kliyo in a military jeep, the hood emblazoned with the symbol of the Kingdom. He stood up, and she slowed to a stop, her lips pursed but one corner of her mouth turning up.

"Don't say it," Cavan told her.

"Which thing?" her lower voice asked, the other two harmonizing. "The part about you shouldn't go off alone in the Badlands, or the part about you shouldn't go off alone in the Badlands without communications and with limited ammo?"

"Both of those things."

She waited while he climbed into the jeep. "You look like hell, Lieutenant."

"What a coincidence."

Kliyo nodded toward the glove compartment. "I brought you some Witches' Brew."

Cavan hesitated. "What?"

"You heard me."

Witches' Brew was the colloquial name for a powerful - and rare - healing potion that the Grand Coven cooked up exclusively for the use of the royal family. He had seen it during creation, for he'd been raised in the Coven, but he had never had occasion to use it. He'd never thought he would.

"I ought to leave it for Sebastian."

"The Prince won't need it," she predicted. "You do. And what help will you be to him when you're completely broken?"

He opened the glove compartment and found three vials filled with a golden liquid that glowed softly, illuminating the box. If it had been after dark, the glow would have lit up the entire passenger area. He took one of the vials and uncorked it.

"Cheers," he said. Kliyo nodded, and he drank it down.

The taste was like citrus and honeyed whiskey at the same time, and it was viscous in texture, like drinking syrup. He could feel the potion sliding down his throat, and the warmth from it spread through his battered body. Everywhere the magical heat reached, healing followed, and by the time he had finished the entire vial, all of his injuries had been repaired.

Kliyo watched the transformation with approval. "Yes," her higher voice said lightly. "You look better with skin. There was a sandstorm overnight. I'm guessing you were too clocked out to notice."

He recapped the vial. "Yeah. Looks like."

She turned and faced the road, her hands on the wheel. "Where is he?"

"Up ahead, and then turn north." He sat back and buckled in. "I think they're headed to Kristal."

"Well, then. We need to get to them before they get there. Let's go." She downshifted, and the jeep spat gravel as it roared away.

CHAPTER THIRTEEN

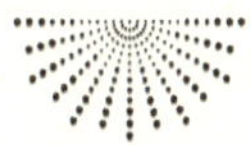

SEBASTIAN

Sebastian woke softly, his head still pillowed on Christopher's shoulder. The incubus' arm was warm around him, his hand possessively resting on Sebastian's ribs. His own arm was hooked over his bed mate's waist, and he lay still, enjoying the feeling. This moment, this intimacy, was more precious to him than their sexual escapades could ever be, and he wondered if Christopher felt the same.

The headache he'd been suffering from was finally completely gone, and he was grateful for its absence. It would probably return as soon as someone lied to him again. He hoped that the first one to lie to him wouldn't be the man in his arms. He slid his hand down to Christopher's hip, cupping the star-shaped brand there. It was hot and throbbing, and he wondered if the Countess was looking in on them now, and if she was, whether the Numeans would be coming for them soon.

He wasn't certain where Christopher was taking them. At first Christopher had said he was going back to Numea, then they had agreed to hide themselves in a place called Kristal. He felt like he should have known about this place, but like all of his memories from his former life, they puffed into nothingness when he reached for them. It was maddening, and his frustration with the exercise was growing.

He knew they had to get rid of the van. It was too obvious and unwieldy, and they needed something faster if they were going to elude their pursuers. He had no doubt that somehow, Cavan Waters had survived the pile-up with the Hunters. If he was honest with himself, he had wanted it that way; that was why he'd shot the tire and not the witch himself. The thought of shooting Cavan made his stomach twist, and he knew that there was more to their relationship than just being in the same military unit.

Had they been lovers once? The witch's reactions to him and to his affection for Christopher seemed to indicate it was so. And who else but a lover would be so dedicated? His pain that Sebastian didn't remember him, his solo pursuit out into the Badlands…it was the only answer that made any sense to him.

He wished yet again that he could remember his former life.

Sebastian thought about the possibility of the Countess retrieving them. The idea of going quietly, of being that woman's obedient possession, sickened him. He could never willingly submit to someone he didn't trust. He refused to return to that den of vipers, to be treated like livestock. If he ever went back, it would be to rescue all of the ones like him who were being abused and to burn the Five Cities to the ground. He pressed his hand against the throbbing star on the incubus's hip and addressed his thoughts to the Countess, hoping she could hear him.

No more. Never again.

"You're awake," Christopher said softly. Sebastian looked up at him, and the incubus kissed him with tender lips. "Good morning."

The dragonel smiled. "Good morning."

"Is the sandstorm over?"

Sebastian left the bed, feeling his buttocks still burning from last night's spanking. He lifted the curtain on the window and looked outside. "Yes. Everything is buried."

"Hmm. Including the van, no doubt."

"No doubt."

Christopher sat up and stretched, then rolled his shoulders and neck. "We need a new vehicle, but hopefully that one will get us as far as Kristal."

Sebastian turned to face him, crossing his arms and leaning his shoulder against the window frame. "What's in Kristal?"

Christopher smiled. "What *isn't* in Kristal? It's the only city in the Badlands. It's the place where sellers go to sell and buyers go to buy, and people from the Badlands come to be entertained. Sometimes people from Pentepolis or the Kingdom - adventure tourists - come to Kristal to see the shows."

"Shows?" he echoed. "Like, plays and concerts and things?"

"There are those," Christopher allowed. "But the gladiators are the most popular show in town."

Sebastian frowned. "Gladiators."

"Yes. The Ludus Kristalia and the Ludus Mysterium go head to head in gladiatorial battles every day, twice on weekends." He shrugged. "They're professional fighters, and they put on a good display."

"Do they fight to the death?"

Christopher looked surprised. "Of course."

"That's barbaric."

"It is, but it's the best-paying job in Kristal, if you can get it. I've often thought that if I ever broke away from the

Countess, I might go there to make a fortune before I went home."

Sebastian sat down gingerly, careful of the handprints on his buttocks. "You're not a fighter."

"Don't underestimate me. I was trained in many things by Lord Ashmar."

The dragonel tilted his head in curiosity. "Where is home for you? Is Hell a real place?"

"It is, and that's where I was born."

"Are you going back there?"

"Not with you in tow." Christopher slid out of bed. "I would never take you there. It would be worse for you than Numea."

"That's hard to believe."

"Oh, believe me. There are worse places than GenTel." He padded toward the bathroom. "Shower?"

"You go ahead."

The incubus turned back to face him, and his eyes were flinty. "It wasn't a request, dragonel."

He felt compelled to follow Christopher, to obey, but he grappled that compulsion and stayed put. The incubus took an angry step toward him, but then he stopped. His expression smoothed, all anger wiped away from his face, seemingly by conscious effort. He shrugged and spoke in a deceptively casual tone.

"Suit yourself."

Sebastian watched the incubus turn and go into the bathroom, leaving the door open. He heard the shower start. He mulled over the situation and reached a decision that he hoped he wouldn't regret. He sighed and followed him in.

Christopher looked over his shoulder when Sebastian joined him in the little room, and he asked with an arched brow, "Just had to be your idea?"

"Something like that. Listen, I will accept you as my

Master when we're in the bedroom, but the rest of the time? You'd better get used to treating me like a partner. I'm sick of being your prisoner, and I'm not going to play along anymore."

Christopher stepped into the water's spray and peered into Sebastian's eyes. The dragonel could feel the other man's demonic power moving, reaching into him. "Are you sure about that?"

He broke eye contact. "Completely sure. Don't try that again, I'm warning you."

The incubus nodded. "You're warning me?"

"I don't want to turn you over to the Mythrians, but I swear to you, I will do it. I want to be with Christopher, not with the Oppressor." He was amazed by how strong he sounded, and by the amount of conviction in his voice. He was even more amazed by the absolute steel he was finding in himself.

"Are you so certain that's not the same person?"

"It had better not be." He wanted to grab Christopher and shake him. "I am never going to live that way again. Not for you, not for anybody. And I am never going back to Numea unless it's with the might of Mythria at my back. I am not your pet. Not anymore."

The incubus listened to him, and the last of his demonic power faded from his face. He nodded. "I understand."

"Do you?"

"Yes. You've been pushed too far."

Sebastian stepped into the shower. "You're right. And I don't want to be pushed anymore."

In other circumstances, Christopher's gaze would have raked over Sebastian's naked body, prurient and possessive. This time, he offered an incongruous handshake.

"Partners."

Sebastian gripped his hand tightly. "Partners."

The brand in Christopher's palm buzzed, and Sebastian pushed him away, feeling betrayed. The force of his shove flattened the incubus's back against the shower wall. "What are you doing?"

"Nothing!" Christopher pressed his hand against his own skin. "Sometimes he does that."

"Who does what?"

"Ashmar. He pulls."

Sebastian shook his head in annoyance. "What the hell are you talking about now?"

"Incubi feed on energy, as you know, but we also feed on souls. We take them through our palms. These brands - " He displayed the eagles in his palms. "These brands mean that whatever souls I take, and whatever energy I'm in contact with, feed straight to Lord Ashmar."

"He's an incubus?"

"No. He's sold his soul, though, and any energy or power he gains goes to his owner."

"The Countess?"

"Exactly."

Sebastian scowled. "So if I were to take a guess, she thinks you're touching me, and she's getting Lord Ashmar to try to take my soul through you?"

Christopher nodded. "Yes."

"So they can kill me from a distance through you?"

The incubus looked miserable. "Why do you think I always wore gloves before?"

Sebastian took a step back, putting space between them. "We're going to get you another pair."

"I think that's a very good idea." Christopher turned around and pressed his palms against the wall.

His head wasn't aching, so he knew that Christopher wasn't lying, but he still didn't trust the things that he was being told. He looked at the incubus's back, at the way the water followed his scars. The fine, white lines that marred the otherwise perfect tan had been joined by a hundred white spots where the torturer's charges had been inserted beneath his skin. He knew that Christopher had suffered from both the Countess's forces and from the Kingdom's. Nobody was innocent, it seemed.

He stepped closer, sympathy overwhelming his distrust. He kissed Christopher between the shoulder blades.

"They don't deserve you," he said. "We'll find a way to break their hold on your soul."

"That isn't possible," Christopher whispered. "I've been trying for centuries, but sold is sold."

"Did you sell your soul to her?"

He was silent for a long moment, standing there with his palms against the shower wall. It was almost as if he was afraid to move. Finally he whispered his answer, the sound nearly lost in the noise from the water. "No. My mother sold it when I was just a child. I just… agreed to the sale."

"Freely?"

He laughed without mirth. "After torture."

"Then that doesn't count. Your soul belongs to you."

"Then why don't I still have it?"

Sebastian turned him around. "How do you know?"

"Because I can feel that it's gone." He looked into Sebastian's face but didn't try to meet his gaze. The dragonel would have shied away from eye contact, anyway, and they both knew it. It would take a long time before he trusted Christopher enough to look into his eyes again. "Just as surely as I can feel that you still have yours."

"I don't believe you can still be alive if you don't have a soul," Sebastian objected. "It's still in there. It's just in chains, and chains can be broken."

"Spoken like a freedom fighter," Christopher mocked mildly. "Who died and made you a hero?"

He put his hands on the incubus's shoulders and pinned him to the wall. "Who died? The dragonel you knew in Numea."

He remembered the way the gas had changed him, and he remembered how it had felt. Sebastian replicated that feeling in his body, and he began to shift. It was shaky and uncertain at first, but after a moment he was standing in the bathroom in his full draconic form, golden scales shimmering as water sluiced between them. He arched his wings, unable to spread them in the tiny room, and raised his head. The incubus stared in wonder.

-Look on me now, Christopher. Look at who I really am.-

His brain spasmed painfully, and more memories rushed at him like a lightning bolt. He staggered back, his tail thrashing, and Christopher stayed motionless in the shower, stunned into immobility. Sebastian's claws dug into the floor, and he felt his fire rising in his chest, the backlight it provided shining the pattern of his scales onto the bathroom walls.

Christopher found his voice, and he asked, worried, "Sebastian… are you all right? Did the transformation hurt?"

His golden eyes fixed on the incubus, and he remembered being captured the first time and being tortured into compliance. He remembered being broken by Lord Ashmar and his canes, being raped, being beaten, having his brain electrified and his mind assaulted. He remembered the Countess being witness to his suffering and how she'd writhed in delight. He remembered Christopher being there, watching, silent, ready to attend to his injuries after they were done.

He remembered his first trip to GenTel and the farm where he'd been kept in a breeding barn. He remembered the daily visits from other veterinarians, and he remembered the shame of voluntarily supplying them with what they wanted. He remembered obediently breeding with a human female, and he remembered watching her bleeding corpse being dragged from the birthing room after the stillbirth she'd pushed free had torn her apart.

He remembered, now.

He remembered everything.

-Look at me!-

His telepathic voice was as loud as a dragon's roar, and in the shower, Christopher recoiled.

-I said, look!-

The dragonel reared up onto his powerful back legs, his forelegs pressed against the walls and his wings straining against the ceiling. Christopher looked.

-I am Crown Prince Sebastian of the Goxtli Golds, Commander of the King's Talons, Warrior of the Kingdom of Mythria, and I am not your prisoner! On your knees! -

Christopher obeyed, his head bowed before the dragonel. Sebastian raised his head and roared in victory.

CAVAN

THE SOUND of a dragon's roar filled the sky, and Cavan knew that sound. He nearly jumped out of his seat in the jeep, and beside him, Kliyo broke into a wide grin. For once, all three of her voices were in concert.

"Prince Sebastian!" she said, her voices a chorus of delight. "He's calling!"

Cavan could hardly believe what he was hearing. "He remembers…. Step on it!"

"I don't even know where we're going yet," her highest voice complained.

Sebsatian roared again, and Cavan homed in on the sound. "Northeast, five degrees."

She nodded and dragged the vehicle off-road, heading in a beeline toward the sound of their prince. Cavan held on, wondering what had caused Sebastian to roar but overjoyed to have heard it. The beaten, submissive slave who had returned from Numea would never have made that call. Sebastian had to have taken his dragon form, which meant that he might have regained his memory.

Cavan had to see for himself.

CHAPTER FOURTEEN

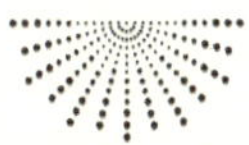

SEBASTIAN

Christopher was shaking. "Your Highness…"

He pulled himself back into his human form. "Don't speak to me," Sebastian commanded. "Don't even fucking look at me."

The incubus obeyed. Sebastian shoved him out of the shower and used the water, himself, trying to wash his shame away. The tingling in his buttocks told him just how far he'd allowed himself to sink, and he angrily scrubbed all traces of Christopher from his body. The incubus retreated into the room, where there was pounding on the door. Dust from the ceiling plaster lay on the bathroom floor, broken free by the dragonel's wings, and it stuck to the incubus's feet as he backed away.

"S-sir?" the desk clerk's voice called, carrying his panic into the room, audible over the hiss of the shower. Sebastian shut off the water and grabbed a towel, wrapping it around his waist. He went to the door, pointing an aggressive finger at Christopher and warning him away from it. Again, the incubus obeyed.

Sebastian yanked the door open, startling the human who

was standing there. The man looked up at him. "S-sir?" he repeated. "Is… is everything all right?"

"Do you have communications here?" Sebastian demanded.

"A telephone, sir, and a short-wave radio."

"Take me to it."

He spared a moment to put his uniform back on, and to use the bungee cords to tie Christopher to the bed while the human clerk looked on in barely-contained panic. He was still stricken by the sound of Sebsatian's roar. Dragons, even dragonels, had a powerful effect upon the minds of simple men.

When he was ready, he nodded to the clerk, who bolted down the hallway toward the office. Sebastian stalked along behind him, his shoulders hunched in his anger. He could feel the gas bladder beneath his spine filling, ready for a fight, responding to his rage. Sebastian forced himself to breathe normal human breaths. He didn't want to set the place on fire.

The office door was wide open when he got there, and the human was pulling disparate pieces of a field radio out of a cupboard. The phone on the front desk was old, but the indicator lights were on, showing the dragonel that there was a connection there, or at least power. He took the field radio out of the man's hands.

"Give me that before you break it."

The man surrendered it without a fight and backed away.

"Please," he sniveled. "I have a family."

Sebastian nodded. "Then go to them. Now."

He didn't watch the man run away. Instead, he assembled the field radio quickly and twisted the knobs, listening to what the rest of the world had to say.

He remembered that the Numean army used frequencies in the high bands, and that the Hunters, when they would broadcast, occupied the mid-range. The Kingdom's forces rarely used conventional communications, but when they did, their equipment worked on the lower frequencies. He listened to the upper bands first. There was silence, which seemed unnatural to him, since there was a Numean presence in the Badlands. The Hunters were chattering, but they were all around Kristal, preparing for another run on felids and lupen, the bread and butter of their sales to the Five Cities. They had found a denning site, and a few of the Hunters were talking about raiding for the cubs. Sebastian frowned and made note of it, hoping that perhaps he could do something to stop them.

The Hunters were his secondary concern. The Numean silence was bothersome. The other cities relied on the Numean forces to protect their interests, and most of the Hunters were virtually owned by the Countess. He also knew that Millennia and Kevdon sometimes sent out raiders of their own. There was no sound from those groups, either. It was as if all of Pentepolis was under radio silence.

He turned the dial down to the lowest register next, and he listened. There were routine sounds from Zyros, the Kingdom's forward operating base on the Badlands frontier: patrols reporting in, intra-base chatter, the idle conversation of the sentry towers. They were relaxed, which told him that Azanel and his people hadn't reached them yet. It sounded like they didn't even know that they were coming.

Sebastian turned off the radio and rifled through the office. He found a Numean rifle and two boxes of ammunition, as well as a uniform, a first aid kit and a military rations bag. These could have been left behind by a patrol, or by a Numean deserter. It was also possible that the clerk he had just released was not as innocent as he appeared. The dragonel dismissed the second possibility. He doubted anyone could replicate the levels of cowardice that man had shown.

He gathered up the Numean articles and found some latex cleaning gloves in a closet. He added the field radio to his booty and took them back to the room.

Christopher was still lying silently where he'd left him, the bungees still intact as if he hadn't tried to escape. Even after Sebastian closed the door, he didn't move. He kept his eyes closed and his face completely blank, and his whole attitude was one of waiting. Waiting to be tortured, perhaps, or waiting to be killed. Sebastian wasn't going to torture him, and when he looked on the incubus's face, other memories bucked inside of him, and he knew he wasn't going to kill him, either. Just what he was going to do was a mystery.

He put down the objects he had appropriated and walked over to where the incubus was lying, still naked and wet from the shower. Christopher did not react.

"Open your eyes."

He silently obeyed.

"Two rules."

The incubus nodded and asked, "What are they?"

"One: If you ever use your powers against me in any way, I will use mine on you, and we both know that won't end well for you. Two: If you so much as twitch in a way that makes me think you're going to betray me, I will end you. Understand?"

He nodded again. There was deep sorrow in his face. "I understand."

"Good." Sebastian released the bungee cords and tossed them aside, and Christopher stared at the dragonel warily. "Now get up and get dressed. We're leaving."

Christopher swung his legs over the side of the bed and rose, rubbing at his wrists. He kept his gaze down on the floor. "Heading for the Kingdom?"

There was bitterness in the incubus's voice, and Sebastian was annoyed to hear it. Christopher had no right to object if the dragonel chose to take him as a prisoner, not after everything that had happened over the last year. He tamped down that irritation, though, and answered in a level tone.

"No. For Kristal." Christopher's eyes snapped up to Sebsatian's face, and he admitted, "I need more intel first before I decide where we're going." He gestured toward the pile of things he had put on the dresser. "There are clothes there for you."

The incubus walked to the pile, and Sebastian picked up the rifle he had brought from the van. He didn't want to admit it, but he wanted to have his firearm handy in case his companion made a move for the other gun. Christopher just put the Numean rifle aside and set about examining the clothing.

"A Numean uniform," he said at last.

"Yes."

"I don't want to wear that."

"I don't care."

He opened his mouth to say something else, but he clearly thought better of it. Instead, he pulled on the latex gloves and started getting dressed. With his head still down, he asked, "Do you want to bind me again?"

"Do I need to?"

He looked at Sebastian, and the dragonel kept his face hard. Christopher sighed. "No."

"Good. Let's go." He gestured with his rifle, and they walked out to the van together. Sebastian pointed at the wheel. "You drive."

Christopher raised an eyebrow. "You'd trust me not to take you back to Numea?"

"Yes, because I remember the way to Kristal, and if you deviate, I'll shoot you in the fucking head."

He didn't expect the look of pained betrayal that flickered

over the incubus's face. It made him almost regret his words. Christopher turned to look straight ahead.

"I need the keys."

Sebastian tossed them to him. "Drive."

His former captor drove. They rode in silence, and they had only been on the road for a few minutes when the side-view mirror showed Sebastian a jeep speeding their way. He recognized the insignia on the hood.

"Fuck," he muttered.

He left his seat and climbed into the back of the van so he could see their follower more clearly. He recognized Kliyo at the wheel, and Cavan sitting beside her. Sebastian was pleased to see Cavan looking whole and healthy, and he tried to hide his relief. He turned to look at Christopher, and the sight of the incubus made him feel conflicted. He swallowed the uncomfortable feeling.

"Stop the van."

Christopher looked into the side mirror and Sebastian knew he saw the Kingdom jeep, too. The incubus sighed and clenched his jaw in agitation and possibly fear. The van rolled to a stop, and Christopher stayed motionless with both hands on the wheel, his shoulders slightly slumping. Sebastian could sense the feeling of defeat and loss that filled his companion. He spoke softly.

"I'm not giving you up, Christopher. Don't be afraid."

The other man looked at him through the rearview mirror, surprised. Sebastian meant to say more, though he didn't know what, but the jeep roared up and Cavan leaped out before he could.

"Commander!" Cavan called. His voice caught on the word, and Sebastian pushed open the van's rear doors. He climbed out into the sunlight, and the witch stopped short, his eyes bright. Kliyo also left the vehicle and stood by the front hood, her arms crossed.

Sebastian crossed the space between them and grabbed Cavan in a massive hug, his arms squeezing the witch as closely as he could. Cavan embraced him back, his lips against Sebastian's ear.

"Do you…?" he began to ask.

The dragonel whispered, "I remember. I remember everything."

Impulsively, he kissed Cavan deeply. Best friend, colleague, patrol partner…lover. Cavan made a small sound in his throat, then kissed him back, his hands gripping the fabric of Sebastian's uniform. They broke the kiss but not the embrace, and Kliyo respectfully gave them a moment of privacy. Christopher, watching through the vehicle's mirrors, stayed in the van.

Cavan pulled back reluctantly. "Are you back? I mean, really back?"

"I think so." He smiled for him. "Are you hurt?"

"I was." The witch punched him in the shoulder. "You shot my bike out from under me, you shithead."

Sebastian's smile widened. "It was a really good shot."

Kliyo stepped forward at that moment, and Sebastian embraced her, as well. She patted his back and squeezed him in her arms before she pulled away, grinning. "It's so good to see you as yourself, Seb. What about…?"

The dragonel turned and squared his stance, ready for objections. "Christopher, come on out. He's not the person you both think he is."

Cavan frowned. "The hell he's not. Everything he did at GenTel…"

"Was against his will." He looked at his two companions as the incubus climbed out of the van. "His mother sold his soul to the Countess. He was as much a prisoner as I was… and still is."

The witch scoffed, "How can you sell someone else's

soul?"

"He was a child. His parent had the right," Kliyo answered quietly. "But when he became an adult, it would have reverted to him."

The incubus walked slowly toward them. His face was neutral, but Sebastian could see the warring emotions in his eyes. "Lord Ashmar tortured me into agreeing to the sale," Christopher told them bleakly.

"So am I supposed to feel sorry for you?" Cavan asked harshly.

"No. I don't want your pity. My sins are my own."

Sebastian interjected, "No. You know as well as I do that the Countess and Lord Ashmar forced your hand." He turned and looked into Cavan's bright green eyes. "Christopher is my partner now. We're in this together… all four of us."

The witch looked irritated, if not angry, and Kliyo put her hand on his shoulder. "And what exactly are we in?"

"Azanel is plotting something, I'm sure of it. We need to find out what, and then we need to stop it," Sebastian answered. "And when that's done, we need to go back to GenTel to free our people and save my children. But first we're going to Kristal to regroup and resupply. The Hunters are also planning a raid on a lupen denning site, and I'd like to disrupt that if we can."

"Ambitious as always." Kliyo nodded and gestured toward the van. "Leave that rattletrap behind. We can all fit in the jeep, and it'll go faster in case we run into Hunters."

"If?" Cavan asked wryly. "The closer we get to Kristal, the more Hunters we're going to see, especially with this asshole sparkling like a glitter ball."

Sebastian looked down at his skin, exposed where he had rolled up the sleeves of his uniform. His scales caught the sunlight and glinted brightly. He rolled the sleeves back down. "Fine." He held out a hand to Christopher. "Are you coming?"

The incubus looked at him and spoke in his mind, his mental voice redolent with resentment. -- *Are you actually giving me the choice?--*

Sebastian dropped his hand. *--You're a fine one to bitch about choices, but yes. Come with me, Christopher. Let me save you from the Countess, too.--*

--I thought you hated me now.--

--I was angry,-- he defended. *--I had just remembered every-thing, but trust me... I don't hate you. But I have the right to be angry.--*

- And are you still angry now?-

He answered honestly. *-I'm going to be angry for a very long time.-*

Christopher looked down and said, "We need to get our gear."

Cavan reached into the van and grabbed the things they'd brought from the hotel, and he took a quick look through the rest of the van's contents. He grabbed a few more things and threw the whole accumulation into the back of the jeep.

"Right," the witch said. "Let's go."

Sebastian climbed into the jeep's back seat and pulled Christopher in with him. Cavan watched them in irritation, but he returned to the passenger seat while Kliyo once again took the wheel. She fired up the engine, and the three men fell into a stony silence.

As she drove, Kliyo looked at her companions. She shook her head and muttered sarcastically, "This is going to be fun."

CHAPTER FIFTEEN

SEBASTIAN

They smelled the city before they saw it. A heavy layer of smog surrounded Kristal, whose steel-framed walls were stained with rust and less savory substances. The metal panels were pockmarked with countless bullet holes, and the stench of open sewers assaulted Sebastian's nose like a fist.

"Mm, Kristal," Cavan commented. "The most misnamed city in the world."

Kliyo chuckled. "It was named after the man who founded it, Oleg Kristal. He was from Pentepolis."

"What city?" Christopher asked quietly.

"Sovina, I think," she mused, her upper voice humming instead of forming the words. "I don't really remember. It doesn't matter, though. If there's any presence here from the Cities, it's from Numea... as you no doubt know perfectly well."

Cavan turned in his seat and looked at Christopher. "Feel free to cough up any information about that, by the way."

"Your people already tortured all of my information out of me," the incubus said bitterly. "Wasn't that on your tablet?"

"Yeah, probably, but I sent that back to the Kingdom along with Azanel," Cavan told him. "He'll probably recover from that head injury you gave him, by the way."

Christopher looked out at the approaching city. "More's the pity."

Sebastian laughed quietly. Kliyo glanced at him and asked, "So… about that Mate thing…"

"Lies," he answered firmly. Both Cavan and Christopher looked pleased with that answer, and he noted their reactions with some amusement. Things could be very interesting if he played his cards right.

"So what happened that weekend?" she asked. "Right before the mission that went so sideways?"

Sebastian took a deep breath and thought back. He had multiple memories of the event, and the combination was confusing. The harder he tried to remember, the more confused he got. He frowned and rubbed his forehead with his fingertips.

"I…"

Pain exploded in his head, and it felt like someone had hit him in the face with an axe. He gasped and grabbed the nearest thing he could reach, which happened to be Christopher's knee. The incubus moved toward him, but Sebastian's eyes were closed tightly against the agony. He heard a voice calling his name, but he couldn't recognize it. He tried to breathe, but his chest constricted around his pounding heart.

He didn't know who he was.

-*Sebastian,*- Christopher's voice said in his mind. -*Breathe.*-

He knew that voice, and it brought him solace in the storm. Sebastian. He remembered being called that. Was that really his name? Or was it a name his Master had given him? Nothing made sense.

-*I… I can't…*-

Three women spoke at once. "What's wrong with him?"

His Master answered, "It's the neural editing trying to reassert itself."

A man snapped, "What do you mean?"

"Exactly what it sounded like," Christopher answered testily. "I'll explain the science later, if you think you can grasp it."

"Boys," the women scolded.

Christopher's fingers gently massaged Sebastian's temples, and he could feel energy being wicked away. The more the incubus took, the calmer his mind became, until the dragonel sagged into the seat, virtually sedated.

"There," Christopher said softly. "Open your eyes."

Sebastian did as he was told. His Master was kneeling on the seat beside him, his dark eyes filled with compassion. His hands dropped to the dragonel's shoulders, and Sebastian brought his own up to grasp Christopher's wrists, holding them like a lifeline. The incubus kissed him on the forehead.

"It's all right now," Christopher told Sebastian.

"The hell it is," the other man objected. Sebastian looked at him, slowly realizing that he was riding in a vehicle. The man had a handsome face, with blond hair and pure green eyes, their beauty only slightly marred by the fear he saw there. "Sebastian, are you okay?"

"He will be."

"I wasn't asking you, Oppressor."

Christopher growled over his shoulder. "That's not my name, and I'm the only one who can help him now."

The women - no, one woman with a strange, tripartite voice - was sitting at the wheel, staring back at them. The vehicle wasn't moving. "How?" she asked.

"I'll explain when we can get him somewhere safe. He needs to rest."

"I..." Sebastian started.

"Don't argue."

"Yes, sir."

The other man straightened in his seat with a disgusted exhalation. Sebastian felt as if he'd done something very wrong, but he didn't know what that might be. He looked anxiously into Christopher's eyes, and his Master shook his head.

-Don't worry about him. Just concentrate on breathing.-

"My head," he winced.

"I know. The pain is considerable, but it will pass."

The man in the front seat snarled, "I blame you."

Christopher responded angrily. "I tried to stop them. I told them they were going too far."

"Was that your professional opinion as a veterinarian?" the man sneered.

"As a matter of fact, it was. My opinion as a *doctor*."

Sebastian shook his head, rocking it back and forth on the headrest of his seat. He wanted to beg them to stop arguing, because it made the pain worse, but he wasn't certain if he would be punished if he spoke out of turn. He didn't know where he was or where they were taking him, but he trusted Christopher... mostly. At least he was someone he knew. He wanted to take his hand, but he knew better than to take such liberties without permission, so he clenched his fist in his lap instead.

Christopher seemed to know what he wanted, for he took Sebastian's hand in his, holding it tightly. The grip was a comfort, and he clung to it as the vehicle began to move again. The woman spoke quietly to the man in the front seat, speaking a language that the dragonel didn't understand. He felt he should have known what they were saying, but he couldn't wrap his head around it. He only knew that he was in utter, skull-splitting agony.

Beside him, Christopher whispered to him, coaching him

to take calming breaths. He tried to obey, but weariness filled him and made it difficult to resist the pain. He turned his face toward his Master and fell away into darkness.

~

CAVAN

THE SOUTHERN GATE WAS CLOSED, so they continued around the walls to the gate on the east. The walls were necessary to keep the Hunters out and to protect the city from the other depredations of the Badlands, but they also had the effect of containing Kristal's growth. The population had tried to build upward, but a lack of qualified architects and one too many collapses had inspired the people to dig down instead, creating warrens beneath the surface. The richest people in Kristal lived above the smog line, and the poorest lived underground. Cavan wondered if there was a spare cavern where he could wall Christopher up and leave him.

He turned in his seat and looked at Sebastian, lying unconscious on the Oppressor's shoulder. Christopher, wearing ridiculous latex gloves, was holding his hand, and he looked up at Cavan with a challenging air. The witch turned around again, his jaw set.

Kliyo spoke to him again in his people's ancient tongue, her voices in quiet concert. "This is only temporary. He'll come back to us."

Cavan nodded, appreciating what the moira was trying to do. Knowing her species' ability to take limited looks into the future, he should have been comforted. He wasn't.

They joined a group of vehicles waiting to be allowed

entry through Kristal's eastern gate. Two sentries, massive half-minotaur cryptomorphs with flowing black manes, stood beside the gates while a pack of lupen soldiers surrounded each vehicle in turn. When they reached the front of the line, the wolf shifters swarmed the jeep, their entire pack sniffing at the vehicle while pointing their rifles casually at the four faces inside. Cavan gave a death stare to the lupen at his window, and the man snickered.

The lupen by Kliyo's door said, "Three Kingdom soldiers with a Numean? Is he your captive?"

"Something like that," she answered, her middle voice loud and her other two voices barely speaking. She was doing her best to sound human, and even though Cavan gave her full points for the attempt, she was failing.

"What brings you to Kristal?"

"Personal business."

The lupen doing the interrogating leaned over to look into the backseat again. "What's the matter with him?"

"He's tired," Christopher said.

"Do I know you?" the soldier asked Christopher, his eyes narrowed.

Cavan wanted to throw Christopher under the bus more than he'd ever wanted anything, but he held his silence. Kliyo said, "I don't know how you would. This man is a deserter from Numea and this is his first time in the Badlands."

The lupen snorted. "Deserter, huh?" He scanned the incubus in the back seat. "What's with the gloves?"

"He's a germaphobe."

"Right." He sounded less than convinced, but he stepped back. One of his pack members yipped at him, and he nodded. "And exactly why should we give you access to our city? What's in it for us?"

Christopher turned and reached into the back of the jeep,

grabbing something out of the gear they'd stowed there. It was the field radio.

"Here. That should be worth the cost of admission."

Cavan began to object, but the lupen took the radio and looked it over. After a while, he nodded and held the offering up in one hand so his pack could see it. They yipped in approval. He turned back to the occupants of the jeep with a wry smile.

"First time in the Badlands, huh?"

Christopher set his jaw. "I read."

He laughed. "Whatever. Go ahead."

"Thank you," Kliyo smiled. She drove slowly through the gate, nodding at the minotaur-men as they passed. One of them nodded back, his horns gleaming in the sunlight. Behind them, the lupen they'd spoken to began to fiddle with the radio. Cavan wiped the sweat from his palms and hoped for the best.

When they were safely inside the gate and on the edge of the chaos that was Kristal, Christopher asked, "Germaphobe?"

"It sounded plausible," she shrugged. "What was I supposed to say? I don't even know why you're wearing the damned things."

Sebastian groaned, and Christopher turned his attention immediately to the dragonel. The incubus' face was full of concern for the man beside him, and it annoyed Cavan to no end. He wanted to say that it was because he distrusted Christopher so much, but he knew jealousy when he felt it. He kept his teeth clenched and his mouth shut.

"Sebastian?" Christopher asked, his voice soft.

The dragonel straightened and put his hands over his face. When he answered, he sounded stronger, but he was clearly still in pain. "Yeah."

"Are you all right? How's your head?"

"It feels like someone's trying to jackhammer it open from the inside."

"Sounds unpleasant," Kliyo commented. She glanced at Cavan.

"It is." Sebastian looked around them while their driver bravely maneuvered into the crowded streets. "Kliyo. Cavan. Where are we?"

"Kristal," Cavan told him. "Badlands."

"I know where Kristal is. Why are we here?" He groaned. "Ugh, why does my head hurt so bad? Did someone cold-cock me?"

He sounded like the old Sebastian, and Cavan let himself hope. Christopher was the one who answered the question.

"You had a neural editing relapse. It seems to have passed for now, but there will likely be more in the future. I wish we had access to proper medical equipment. I'd like to do a cranial scan to make sure there are no bleeds."

"Professional curiosity, or just pulling the wings off flies?" Cavan asked. "When we stop, I can take a look at him."

Kliyo nodded. "Well, priorities. I'll pull over."

"Not here, you won't. We'll all be killed and the jeep chopped down for parts before you can even dismount the vehicle," Cavan objected. "If we can make it into the green zone, we can stop then."

He turned in his seat and reached a hand out to Sebastian. The dragonel accepted it readily, his scales smooth and cool to the touch. It was a good sign that his fire wasn't burning; it meant that he didn't feel threatened. Cavan closed his eyes, using his OtherSight to check Sebastian for injury. He saw nothing that his witchcraft could recognize as a problem, and he opened his eyes, still holding Sebastian's hand.

"No physical damage. It's probably a hiccup in the neurotransmitters or something. I can't see on that level."

The incubus nodded. "That's a relief. Thank you for checking."

Cavan's gaze locked with Christopher's. He carefully warded his vision as a precaution, preventing any mental manipulation that the other man might try to do. To his credit, Christopher's demonic powers remained quiescent.

"You're welcome. He's a little important to me."

"As he is to me."

Sebastian looked from one man to the other, and he said, "You're both…"

Kliyo interrupted him. "I think we're going to have trouble getting to the green zone."

"Why?" Cavan asked.

He looked out the windscreen and got his answer. Up ahead of them, a massive truck, rusted out and a disgrace to all things automotive, had toppled onto its side. It was blocking both lanes of the highway, spilling its cargo. A huge group of scavengers were looting the thing, carrying off whatever wasn't nailed down, including the driver.

"We should stop them," Sebastian said.

"With all due respect, Seb, this is Kristal," Cavan told him. "Looting is par for the course, and kidnapping in broad daylight is sort of the official sport around here. If we get involved, we're outnumbered by about a hundred to one. If we go after them, we'll just be added to their catch. Besides, you're a pretty prime kidnap prize… in case you've already forgotten."

Sebastian pressed his lips into an unhappy line and fell silent. Beside him, Christopher nodded. "He's right. We need to just go around and hope they don't notice us. This jeep is in better condition than most of the other things I've seen on the road here. I'm sure they'd love to get their hands on it."

Kliyo threw the jeep into reverse just as the looters noticed them idling there. A trio of men with heavy crowbars in their hands split off from the main group and headed in their direction.

"Not today, guys," Kliyo mumbled, putting on some speed. She reversed all the way down the block until she reached a cross street flanked by half-collapsed hovels with stretched tarps for roofs. She turned and drove quickly away from the crash site, heading for the center of town.

Sebastian looked at the city as they went by. The houses were little more than huts made of scrap metal and tarp, stacked haphazardly on top of one another and choking in the smog. There were people of every conceivable kind, but they all shared the same hungry, hopeless look. He shook his head. "Why do they live this way?"

"Because any life inside the city walls is better than life outside it," Cavan answered. "The Badlands are no place to raise a family."

"But why not rise up?" the dragonel asked. "Why not fight for a way to make things better?"

Christopher replied quietly, "For most people, it's difficult to find the will to fight when just existing is exhausting. These people wouldn't be here if they had a choice, and they wouldn't be living this way if there was another option. But the Hunters run this place, and they crush these people beneath their heels."

Sebastian narrowed his eyes. "And who runs the Hunters?"

Kliyo was the one with the answer this time. "The strongest of them rule the rest. There is a group of five, the original Hunters who were hired by the Countess, and they hold the reins of control."

"Only five?"

"With legions of followers and hangers-on." Cavan shook his head. "I can see where your train of thought is going, and please don't. We have enough trouble without you getting all righteous."

Sebastian fell silent, but Cavan knew him well enough to know what he was thinking. For most of his life, Sebastian had been sheltered, a pampered princeling in the Golden Hall. He'd grown up on fairy tales and military propaganda, and he really believed that goodness would always win the day. The dragonel had been obsessed with justice for as long as Cavan had known him, and despite his soft upbringing, Sebastian had more fight in him than anyone the witch had ever known. It was part of why Cavan loved him so. He knew that if he let him, Sebastian would try to start a revolution. While that was certainly needed in a place like Kristal, it was also a fool's game, because too many people were benefiting from the status quo. They wouldn't take kindly to a mythric's meddling.

They drove out of the shanty town and into an area that had better buildings and neater streets. Ahead was another checkpoint manned by felid soldiers, and they slowed to a halt outside the green zone.

Kliyo stopped the vehicle and waited while the pack surrounded them. Their leader stepped up to the driver's side door.

"State your business," he said, his tenor voice clear and smooth.

"We request entry to the green zone."

"Why?" He leaned forward and scanned the occupants. When his ice-blue eyes hit Sebastian, he broke into a smile. "Well, I'm impressed. Is Prince Sebastian your companion or your prisoner?"

The dragonel was shocked. "You know me?"

"Don't you know me?" the lupen challenged. He was half-shifted into his wolf form, his eyes feral and his ears long and pointed. Multiple piercings graced those ears and his septum, and his long blond hair was elaborately braided with more brass rings. He leaned over to look into the backseat again.

Sebastian leaned forward, and Cavan peered at his face. Recognition sparked in the witch's mind, and he blurted out, "Lupul? Is that you?"

"Lt. Waters," he nodded.

Clearly, Sebastian remembered him, too. He spat, "Deserter."

"Better than serving the dragons," Lupul countered.

"Prince Sebastian is my prisoner," Christopher said.

Cavan turned and stared at the incubus, fighting the urge to punch him in the face. Lupul grinned. His teeth were sharp, filed into points. "Is that a fact?"

"It's a fact."

The lupen looked at Cavan. "And you're going along with it? I highly doubt that. You're lying."

Kliyo spoke up, her three voices firm and harsh. "Lt. Waters is our prisoner as well. He's under compulsion."

"A compulsion." His tone was flat. He didn't believe a word he was being told.

"Yes," Cavan agreed. "You know that the moirae can control witches."

"Do I?"

Kliyo spoke, and this time her voices were hollow and echoing. Power moved through that sound, and it filled the jeep with menace. "I am sister to the Fates, and magic flows through us. Witches owe their power to me and to my sisters, and what we give, we can take away. We also give the shifters the power to take their animal forms. Let us pass, or I will show you what happens when the choice to shift or not is taken from you."

Lupul took an instinctive step backward. He glanced at his pack, who had also sensed the threat and had retreated. He took another step away and waved them through.

"On your way." He turned to his packmates. "Open the gate."

The metal barrier slid aside, and Kliyo wasted no time driving through. They left the checkpoint behind and drove deep into the green zone, where the landscape changed abruptly. All around them, neatly-manicured lawns of actual grass, with flower beds and trees, gave the area its name. Cavan could smell the magic on the vegetation, which should never have been able to survive in a wasteland. The people in charge lived well, that was certain.

"That son of a bitch should be in chains," Sebastian snarled. "We need to find a good place to stop."

"I'm working on it," Kliyo answered. Only her middle voice formed the words. The others, perhaps spent from the effort of releasing her power, were silent. It was strange to hear only one voice from her.

"Good," the dragonel said. "My head is pounding."

Cavan looked at Christopher, whose face was grim. "I'm sure it is," the incubus said. "The neural editing is something that's hard to overcome. But there is a way."

Anger flashed through the witch. He was angry that the neural editing had been done at all, that the one responsible for it was sitting so calmly at his lover's side, and that he himself was unable to do a damned thing about any of it. He warned, "You'd better do it, and fast."

Christopher looked at Cavan and narrowed his eyes. "I know what to do. The question is, are you willing to help?"

"I'd do anything for him."

"And so would I."

"If you guys could stop fighting over me for a minute, that would be awesome," Seabstian sighed. "Whatever our next step is, we need to take it together. We can't have any division between us. Understand?"

Kliyo nodded, and Cavan backed down. "I understand," he said.

Christopher looked away. "I understand."

"Good, because it's just the four of us against the world, and I don't like those odds." The dragonel closed his eyes and leaned his head back on the seat. "We have a lot of work ahead of us."

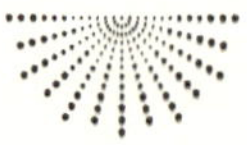

CHAPTER SIXTEEN

He opened his eyes and regretted it immediately. He had never had a headache as horrible as the one that was afflicting him now, and the bright lights of the room he was in were purely murder. A soothing hand touched his brow, and a woman's voice spoke in his ear.

"You're going to be all right, Your Highness. Just rest now."

Azanel groaned and raised his hand to his head. His hair was sticky with blood, but the skull beneath it was more or less intact.

"You sustained a serious injury," the woman helpfully told him. "You were struck on your shifting suture and the impact made your brain swell. We were able to bring a witch from Grand Coven in to help you, and there's no permanent damage."

He didn't remember getting hit. The last thing he remembered was going into the room where Sebastian and the Oppressor were sleeping, responding to a call for help, or what he'd presumed was a call for help. He should have known better than to let the dragonel and the incubus stay together. The demon had clearly reestablished his control over Sebastian's mind, and that would not do.

He started to sit up, and the woman put her hand on his shoulder, holding him in place. "Not so fast, sir," she said. "You're healed of the injury, but you still need to rest. There are after-effects that the witches couldn't cure."

Azanel objected, "I need to find the prince."

"Not your job now," she said, "but he will be found."

"I need to find him," he reiterated, pushing her aside.

He forced his eyes open. The woman beside him was a wood nymph, her green hair bound back with vines. She wore the robes of a healer, and her face was gentle and compassionate. It annoyed him and made him feel patronized. The ice dragon pushed her back and sat up, swinging his legs over the side of the bed. Another healer, this one a sylph, rushed over.

"Prince Azanel, please. You will not heal completely if you don't rest."

"I don't have time. I need to find my Mate."

The wood nymph left the room and returned with a tall woman in leather armor. "Prince Azanel, this is Cassandra. She will be seeking out the prince while you recover."

He eyed the newcomer suspiciously. "Who are you supposed to be?"

"She told you. I'm Cassandra." The woman crossed her arms and squared her stance, her movements those of a trained fighter. Azanel disliked her immensely.

"Should that mean something to me?"

The nymphs looked at one another and left the room. Cassandra walked closer to the dragon. "That depends. How well do you know the king?"

He lifted his chin. "Intimately."

"Then you should know my name." She leaned in, her

hands on the bed on either side of his hips. "I'm the king's personal assassin."

Azanel glared into her dark eyes, unwilling to give her the satisfaction of moving away from her. She was trying to intimidate him, and he would stand his ground. "The king doesn't have a personal assassin."

She chuckled. "I guess you're not as close to Goxtli as you thought."

"*King* Goxtli. Unless you believe you're his equal."

"I'm more than his equal, dragon. I'm his superior."

Cassandra backed away, and Azanel hissed, "Nobody is the king's superior."

She laughed. "If you say so. There are others who would disagree."

"They're wrong." He looked around himself. "Where am I?"

"In the healer's compound at Zyros," Cassandra told him. "You very nearly died before those two soldiers you were with could bring you here."

"Only two?"

Cassandra shrugged. "So I'm told."

"What about the king's emissary and the other man?"

"I don't know what you're talking about, nor do I care. Your party and your ability to misplace them is not my concern. What I need to know is where you last saw the prince."

Azanel stood and held the table for stability. Dizziness made him feel as if the entire room was whirling around him. He closed his eyes until the sensation passed. "The Oppressor has taken him in the Badlands."

"The Oppressor?" Cassandra sounded delighted. "Well, that makes all of this so much more interesting. Where in the Badlands?"

"Along the road. There's only one highway between Numea and Zyros."

"Yes, but so many ways to travel without using that road. Still… you've given me some helpful information in spite of yourself."

He hated her. "Then go make use of it. I need to see the king."

"Well, you're in luck, because he's come out here to meet you. He was ever so eager to see his son… I can't imagine that he'll be too thrilled to find out that you lost him."

"Taken," Azanel corrected. "He was taken from me. I was unconscious."

Cassandra laughed. "Yes, I'm sure that will make all the difference to a grieving dragon. They're known for being reasonable."

He glared at her but couldn't find the words to make a rejoinder. He could only glower at her and try to keep from vomiting.

The woman turned her back on him and strolled toward the door. "Don't worry, dragon. I'll find your prize. And maybe I'll even let you keep him when I get back."

She left him alone, and Azanel was pleased to see her leave. He took a deep breath and tried to will the world to hold still, but it would not obey. The wood nymph returned, and she gently put her hands on his shoulders.

"Please, Your Highness. Lie down."

He was in no condition to argue. He went back onto the bed, lying down with his head on the blood-stained pillow. He sighed, and the nymph patted his hand sympathetically.

The other nymph returned, as well, and there was a look of shocked excitement on her face. "He's here!"

"Oh my stars!" the wood nymph exclaimed. She looked around the room in a panic, either looking for somewhere to hide or checking on the presentability of the place.

"Who's here?" Azanel asked.

"The king!"

He had dismissed Cassandra's statement about King Goxtli coming to Zyros as a lie, but apparently she'd been telling the truth. Azanel began to sit up again, but the wood nymph pushed him back down.

"Your Highness, please."

A wave of draconic power swept into the room, and the door opened with a bang. King Goxtli strode in, his ancient blood and undeniable majesty filling the air with the crackling of magic. He was in his human form, but his skin was covered in a sheen of fine golden scales that made him shine like the idol from some exotic shrine. His eyes were molten gold, and his head was bald, shaved to allow the crown scale to show. He stopped short when he saw Azanel, and a trio of armor-clad escorts came in and fanned out around him.

"Prince Azanel," the king said, his voice a deep basso rumble. "Did you see him? Did you see my son?"

Azanel hadn't thought of what he'd say, since he assumed he'd have more time before he saw the king. He thought quickly, remembering the plan that he'd been trying so hard to put into motion, and decided on a course of action.

"I did, Your Majesty."

"And was he..."

"They did something to his mind that erased his memories. He didn't know me." He let his voice drip sorrow, and it had the desired effect on the monarch. King Goxtli swept up to him and put a massive hand on Azanel's shoulder.

"I feared this was the case. My son would have fought them long and hard. They would have to disable him somehow." He paused. "Are his memories gone for good?"

"I don't know, Your Majesty. The only one who knows is the Oppressor."

The king's jaw set, and his sharp teeth ground together. "And where is he?"

Azanel closed his eyes, mostly because he feared the reaction that he was about to get. "He absconded with the prince. The Oppressor is the one who attacked me and left me for dead."

Goxtli stepped back and roared in grief and rage. All around the healer's room, glass vessels shattered under the force of the sonic blast, and Azanel's ears rang. The king finished the roar with a groan, and Azanel risked looking up at him. The king's expression was one of pure anguish.

"How can this be? We were so close to retrieving him. So close to having him home. And now that... *monster*... has stolen my son again!" He clenched his fists. "I will have him in chains! I will break him as he broke my Sebastian!"

"As I continue to live and breathe, I swear that I will do all within my power to make it so."

Goxtli gathered up his emotions and re-established some semblance of self-control. He took a deep breath, and Azanel could hear the muted bubbling sound of the king's gas bladder.

"I know you will. You have lost as much as I in this," the king told him. "What they did to him... did it disrupt your Mate bond?"

Azanel surged with delighted excitement that he struggled to keep from his expression. The king had just handed him the perfect excuse for why he and Seabstian were not truly Mated. He conjured a tear and nodded. "Yes, Your Majesty. The bond is gone."

The king put his hand over his eyes, then hauled in another deep, steadying breath. Finally he dropped his hand and looked at Azanel with compassion.

"You must be suffering so," he said sadly. "I know how I felt when my Mate died and the bond was severed within me. The pain was unbelievable. No wonder you lost contact with him. This must have been a recent development… you were able to reach him for such a long time."

He had acted the part to perfection, and it pleased him that the king was still convinced that he'd had some sort of long-distance psychic insight into Sebastian's wellbeing. The king was firmly convinced of everything that Azanel had said, and he would be a powerful ally when the time came for him to force the Mating bond with Sebastian.

"It is agony," he said softly.

King Goxtli bent and pressed his forehead to Azanel's, the dragon equivalent of a fatherly kiss. "Rest, dear Azanel. You are badly wounded and have suffered greatly. I will have you brought back to the Golden Hall and you'll be treated by the finest healers in all of Mythria."

"Thank you, sir, but I want…"

"To find your love. I know. I want to find him, too. But I trust Kliyo and Lt. Waters, and they are searching for him now. They will find him and bring him home to us."

Azanel disliked leaving anything to those two; they had always been too friendly with Sebastian, especially Cavan, who had too easily fallen into the prince's bed. He would have preferred to be on the search party, too, but he knew that the king was not going to hear of anything of the sort.

"Yes, sir." He closed his eyes. "Thank you, sir."

Goxtli squeezed his hand. "I will send others, people with special skills in searching out the missing. He will not be lost for long." He turned away. "I couldn't bear it."

Azanel listened as the king and his retainers left. He had to plan his next moves very carefully.

CHAPTER SEVENTEEN

SEBASTIAN

hey found a place to stop in the center of the green zone. It was a hotel, and unlike the broken-down shells they'd stayed in out in the Badlands, this one was in good repair. More than that, it was opulent, with a beautiful marble-lined fountain in the lobby. Sebastian was so weary and his head hurt so badly that he was unable to really appreciate it, but he tried to remember to look at it in the morning. The idea of him trying to remember anything filled him with bitter amusement.

Kliyo took control of the situation, checking them into a suite on one of the upper floors. She presented a credit chit with the king's insignia, and there were no questions asked about their motley crew or about their presence in Kristal. Instead, they were ushered to their room with a level of fawning attentiveness that bordered on obsequiousness, the desk clerk recognizing that there were important personages in her presence.

The suite was large and luxuriously appointed, with silk-upholstered furniture and beautifully rendered wooden tables. A crystal chandelier sparkled down from the ceiling in the common room. A bathroom and two bedrooms branched off from the main area, and a kitchenette and a meeting room completed their accommodations. It was more like a condominium than a hotel room.

Sebastian sat down heavily on one of the couches that sat in the middle of the room. Christopher sat beside him. "Head still hurting?" the incubus asked solicitously.

"Like someone's run it over with a truck."

"Sounds unpleasant." Cavan came to stand behind the couch, his hands resting on the sides of Sebastian's head. Pleasant warmth pulsed where the witch touched him, and if the dragonel had been a cat, he would have purred. He closed his eyes to enjoy the comfort that his lover was offering.

Kliyo did a quick check of all the rooms, then joined them. "Can you help him?"

"I can ease the pain," Cavan said. "But I can't stop it from coming back. We have to completely neutralize the neural editing to do that."

"I am so fucking over this," Sebastian growled.

Kliyo looked at Christopher. "What can you do to fix the damage your people have done?"

"There is one thing I can try, but it's risky, and it requires Sebastian's complete cooperation and consent," the incubus said, sounding reluctant.

"Nice of you to take consent into account after all this time," Cavan commented.

Sebastian sighed. "Stop. What do I have to do?"

Christopher looked at Cavan, then back at the dragonel. Something told Sebastian that neither he nor his witch would like what the incubus was about to say.

"I can try to disable the neural editing, but I'll need to be enmeshed with your energy to do it. That means that I can only do this while we're having sex."

Cavan snorted softly. "Convenient."

"You have a part to play in it, too," Christopher told him.

Sebastian narrowed his eyes. "Explain."

"He knows who you were before the editing. If I can enmesh with him at the same time, I can bring your true memories and self - as far as he knows them - to the forefront."

Kliyo chuckled. "Wait. So you're saying you have to have sex with both of them at the same time to do this?"

Christopher answered, annoyed. "I'm an incubus. My power is based in sex. You wanted me to help him, and this is how I can do that."

Sebastian asked, "Will it work?"

"Maybe."

Cavan objected, "That's not good enough."

"I've never done this before," Christopher admitted. "It's the only thing I can think of to do. I'm not exactly well versed in this sort of thing. I want to help, and I can't think of any other way to do it."

"Too bad you weren't as helpful when they were doing this to him."

"I've already said that I tried to stop them. I knew they were going too far."

"Stop it," Sebastian repeated. "Your arguing is making me crazy."

The witch stopped pushing healing energy into Sebastian's head and gripped the back of the couch. "Is there a chance you could make it worse?"

The incubus looked at Sebastian, then looked back at Cavan. "There's always a chance, but I don't think it will happen."

Kliyo shook her head. "It's up to you, Your Highness. This is your risk to take."

He took a deep breath, then asked, "Will it give me back my life?"

Christopher nodded. "It should."

"Should," Cavan echoed derisively.

It was better than nothing, and he was ready to be himself again, without the interference of the Numeans and whatever they had done to him. Sebastian nodded.

"Let's do it."

Christopher looked up at Cavan. "What do you say?"

The witch sighed. "How could I say no?"

Sebastian spontaneously took Cavan's hand and kissed it. "Thank you."

"For you, anything." He touched Sebastian's face, then turned a hard look to Christopher. "If you try to hurt him, or if you use your powers against me in any way…"

The incubus held up his gloved hands. "Stop. I would never hurt Sebastian, and I have no interest in enslaving another witch."

"Another?" Sebastian asked. "The Community enslaves witches, too?"

"The Countess had a witch once," Christopher admitted slowly. "She gave him to me as a companion when she brought me into her household."

"A companion, or a pet?" Kliyo asked quietly.

"Where the Countess is concerned, there's no difference." He sighed and rose from the couch, looking at Sebastian and Cavan. "We should do this soon, because that headache worries me."

"It isn't doing much for my disposition, either." The dragonel stood up and looked at Kliyo. "Please don't go far. If this goes seriously south, we might need you to get help."

She nodded. "I'll be right here."

They walked together into one of the bedrooms with Christopher leading the way. Sebastian closed the door while Cavan stood uncomfortably by the bed. The dragonel turned and looked at the two men, so different in every way but both so important to him. He had no reservations about Cavan. He never had. Their relationship had grown out of friendship and mutual respect, and he knew that if he had a Mate, it was the witch who stood before him now. In fact, he had once broached the subject of such a union with his father, but the king had forbidden it. Sebastian had been obedient and put his own desires aside. He didn't feel like being that cooperative now.

Christopher was a conundrum. Yes, he had done horrible things to Sebastian, and had stood by and allowed others to hurt him as well, but somehow the dragonel forgave him. He believed that the incubus truly cared for him, and that he had been as much a prisoner of the Countess as Sebastian himself had been. Despite everything, he trusted Christopher and believed that there was a kernel of goodness in the incubus's heart. He loved him, even though all logic told him that he shouldn't.

Sebastian wanted them both, and he intended to have them.

"So," Cavan finally said. "This is awkward."

Christopher stripped off his Numean uniform and tossed it into the corner. Sebastian watched Cavan sweep his gaze over the incubus's body, and he smiled.

"He's beautiful, isn't he?" he asked.

Christopher looked up at the dragonel with a smile. Cavan blushed furiously. With a chuckle, Sebastian walked closer until he was standing between his two lovers.

"How do you want to do this?" he asked. "You said you need to enmesh with both of us at the same time. What does that entail?"

Christopher looked at Cavan, then at Sebastian. "I need you both to fuck me at the same time while I do what I can."

Cavan gaped. "Won't that be too distracting for you?"

The incubus spared his rival a smile. "Only if you do it right."

Sebastian put his hand on the back of Christopher's neck and pulled him into a passionate kiss, his tongue sliding into the dark-haired man's mouth. Christopher took a moment to strip his gloves away, and then he buried his fingers in Sebastian's golden hair to kiss him back just as hard. Cavan sighed, and then Sebastian felt his familiar fingers resting lightly on his back. He turned from Christopher and kissed Cavan instead. Their tongues sparred, and Cavan's breath hitched in his throat when Sebastian palmed him through his uniform trousers.

Christopher kissed Sebastian's neck and gently unbuttoned his shirt, kissing down his torso as his skin was exposed. By the time he was kneeling in front of the dragonel, Sebastian's cock was hard and straining against his zipper. The incubus smiled, licked his lips, and released it. His erection sprang free, and Christopher took the tip into his mouth, sucking it gently. Sebastian moaned.

Cavan pulled his own shirt off and tossed it aside. He tried to undo his belt buckle, but his hands were shaking, and he fumbled with it. Sebastian stripped to the waist while Christopher continued to tease him, the tip of his tongue darting like a snake's over the head and into the slit. The incubus released him and set about unlacing the dragonel's boots, kneeling at his feet. Seeing Christopher in such a submissive posture made Sebastian's lust burn hotter, and he ran a possessive hand through the incubus's dark hair.

Cavan finally got his belt undone, and he stripped the rest of the way, not waiting for anyone to help him. His long cock was rampant with need as he kicked his clothes aside. Sebastian used his free hand to stroke him, and he kissed Cavan again.

When they broke to breathe, the dragonel whispered, "Just like old times."

Cavan laughed and cast a glance at Christopher. "Not exactly."

The incubus turned on his knees and took Cavan's cock in his hand, gently pushing Sebastian's hand away, and looked up at him with brown eyes limpid with desire. Cavan nodded to him, and Christopher took him into his mouth, slowly pressing forward until the witch's hot flesh was all the way down his throat. He swallowed around him, and Cavan gasped. Christopher pulled back with a self-satisfied grin.

Sebastian stepped back, stroking himself and watching as the two men he loved most in the world enjoyed one another. Christopher's hard on was hard to ignore, and seeing the incubus going down on Cavan made Sebastian grow harder in his own hand. Cavan touched Christopher's hair hesitantly, and his green eyes flickered up to the dragonel's face as if he was asking if it was all right. Sebastian smiled and leaned over the kneeling incubus to kiss Cavan once again.

He took Christopher's hand and pulled him up from the carpet, leading him over to the bed while Cavan went scavenging for supplies. He returned with bath oil and a look of concern.

"I don't have any condoms," he said.

"Neither do we," Christopher said. "Don't worry about it."

Sebastian grinned at his lover. "You're a witch. In the unlikely event that something ugly takes root, you can take care of it."

Christopher kissed Cavan, and after a moment's hesitation, the witch responded. Sebastian took the oil and poured some onto his fingers. While the two men kissed, he rubbed the oil into Christopher's hole, making sure that it was well lubricated for the challenge it was about to face. He worked the oil into the incubus's body with his fingers, and Christopher broke the kiss to gasp when Sebastian's fingertips found the perfect spot.

"Oh, yes," he moaned.

"Are you going to be able to concentrate?" Cavan asked.

"If not, we'll just have to do it again." Christopher kissed him again.

This time, when their kiss broke, Cavan smiled. "I think I can handle that."

Sebastian pulled his fingers free of Christopher's body and lay down on the bed, oiling his cock in preparation. He handed the bottle to Cavan, who oiled himself up and added more to Christopher. The incubus shivered.

"Not too much," he said. "I don't want you to slip out."

"I don't want to hurt you," Cavan objected.

"Mmm, why not?" Christopher waggled his eyebrows at the surprised witch, and Sebastian laughed.

"You are such a masochist."

"Yes, I am."

Christopher straddled Sebastian and leaned over him, his hands once more in the silken tresses he liked to stroke so much. Sebastian kissed him and guided his cock to Christopher's puckered opening. He breached him slowly, guiding the flared head past the clenching ring of muscle, and Christopher groaned against his mouth.

Cavan moved behind Christopher, and Sebastian spread his legs so that the witch had somewhere to kneel. The dragonel embraced his incubus tightly, holding him chest to chest. He felt the first nudge of Cavan's cock, and the combination of being inside Christopher but being frotted by Cavan was nearly more than he could take. He blew out a steadying breath and tried not to get too carried away. There would be time to do this just for pleasure.

Cavan pushed inside, too, his hardness slotting into

Christopher's body beside Sebastian's. He ran a hand down Christopher's back, and the incubus groaned in pain and pleasure.

"Oh, shit," he breathed.

"Are you okay?" Cavan asked. "Does it hurt?"

"A little," Christopher confessed. "I love it."

Sebastian looked up into Cavan's eyes. "Told you."

Christopher tightened around them, and Cavan's face flushed. He blurted, "You'd better do what you're there to do, because I don't know how long this is going to last."

"Just fuck me," the incubus moaned. "We can do the rest the second time around."

Sebastian grinned. "I like the way you think."

"We all need to nut," Christopher said. "Let's get to it."

Cavan grabbed a handful of Christopher's hair and gave it a yank. The incubus's neck bent back, and the witch began to fuck him. Sebastian moaned at the sensation of sharing Christopher's hole, tight heat and the rubbing making him senseless. Christopher pushed back onto the twin cocks that were impaling him, rocking into their alternating thrusts as Cavan and Sebsatian found their rhythm.

"Oh, fuck," Christopher moaned.

Cavan had hold of the incubus's waist, holding him steady, and Sebastian put one hand over his while his free hand explored the hard nubs on Christopher's chest, tweaking and twisting them. Christopher shuddered, and Cavan cried out, shooting his load into the incubus's well-stretched hole. When Sebastian felt his lover let go, he couldn't hold back any longer, and he came, too.

Cavan pulled out, and Christopher sat back on Sebastian, confining his still-hard cock inside his body. The incubus, not yet satisfied, reached down to stroke himself. Cavan pushed his hand away and replaced it with his mouth. Sebastian kept thrusting into Christopher while Cavan sucked him off.

Christopher cried out, his head falling back onto his shoulders, and Cavan stayed with him the whole time. It was the most amazing thing Sebastian had ever seen, and he came a second time, surprising himself and the incubus who was writhing on his dick.

Cavan pulled away and wiped his mouth with the back of his hand, his eyes dewy with afterglow. Christopher lifted off Sebastian and fell onto the bed, landing between the witch and the dragonel. Cavan looped an arm over him so he could touch Sebastian, and the dragonel held his hand while he pulled Christopher close with the other arm. The witch pressed against Christopher's back and dropped a gentle kiss on the back of his neck. Overcome with satisfaction, all three drifted off into sleep. Christopher's mission hadn't been accomplished, but Sebastian's certainly had.

CHAPTER EIGHTEEN

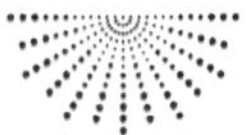

CHRISTOPHER

e woke from his afterglow nap to find Cavan sitting up and awake beside him. On his other side, Sebastian lay quietly with his eyes closed, his breathing deep and even. Christopher rolled onto his back and looked up at the witch.

"Been a while, huh?" he asked, his voice thick with sleep. "I mean, your energy… you haven't had sex in a long time."

Cavan nodded. "Over a year."

Christopher realized what that meant. "You were waiting for him."

The witch nodded again. "I'd wait for him forever if I had to."

"You love him that much?"

"I would die for him."

"Don't do that," Christopher told him. "Live for him instead."

Cavan looked at their sleeping companion, and Christopher could see the depth of emotion in the other man's green eyes. He had to admit that Cavan had a beauty all his own, even if it wasn't as exotic as Sebastian's. There was some-

175

thing familiar about his face, and Christopher had a hard time placing why that was. He would think more about it later.

"What about you?" Cavan asked. "Do you really love him? Are demons capable of love?"

It was a question he had grappled with himself for a very long time. "We are, but in our own way. We're a greedy and avaricious species, and for us, love is more like possession. There are some people or animals or objects that we want to keep as ours and ours alone, and to keep them forever. When that happens, we call it love." He shrugged, unable to put it into better words. "I don't know what love is like for others, but that's how I understand it."

"And what is Sebastian to you? Person, animal or object?"

He sighed. "In the course of the time I've known him, he's been all three."

Cavan's eyes turned hard. "And what is he now?"

"A person. The person I want to spend the rest of my life with."

"For an immortal, that's quite a statement."

"I know. But I mean every word." He took the risk of touching Sebastian's arm, feeling the dichotomy of warm flesh and cool scales. "He's special."

"When did you decide that? While you were raping him, or during the torture?"

He resented Cavan's words, but he knew that he deserved them. "Over the course of his time at GenTel, no matter what they did to him or how many different personalities they tried to force him to have with the neural editing, there were two qualities about him that they never changed, and those were the things that made me love him. He was always brave, and he was always kind."

"In spite of you?"

"Yes. In spite of everything he suffered, he never stopped

caring about what happened to other people, and he never begged for the pain to stop. And there were times that the pain was considerable."

Cavan's voice was cold, and he could feel that the witch was barely holding in his anger. "Pain at your hands?"

"Rarely," he admitted, "but sometimes."

"Then why does he love you?" His tone was filled with desperate confusion and more than a little sorrow.

"I don't know," Christopher said. He looked at the dragonel. "I don't understand it, because I certainly don't deserve it."

"No. You don't."

"Finally we agree on something."

They fell silent, both of them watching their companion. Cavan smiled. "Do you think he's awake and listening to us?"

Christopher chuckled. "Absolutely."

Without opening his eyes, Sebastian said, "Hush. I'm sleeping."

Cavan laughed and threw a pillow at the dragonel, who batted it away. He opened his eyes and smiled, and Christopher thought he had never seen him looking happier.

"You were just going to eavesdrop on our heart-to-heart, huh?"

"It was educational." Sebastian rolled onto his side and kissed Christopher, then sat up to do the same with Cavan. "I have to say, that was amazing."

The incubus grinned. "Tell me about it. I can't wait for round two."

"Do you think you can concentrate this time?" Cavan asked.

"You're obsessed with my focusing. Do you think you can keep from coming in two minutes this time?"

"Hey! It was at least five."

Sebastian laughed. "Three, tops."

"And you were right behind him," Christopher pointed out.

"Right. And it took you a really long time to get there, yourself. Whatever." The dragonel rolled his eyes. "We were all a little needy the first time through, I think. This time we'll be able to sustain it a bit longer… if we're still trying this, that is."

Christopher frowned. "Have you changed your mind?"

"Not at all. Have you?"

"No." He looked at Cavan, who shook his head.

"I wouldn't still be here if I'd changed my mind."

Sebastian lay back down, his hand going to his cock. "Then let's do this, if you're both ready."

"Well, with a romantic proposition like that, how could I resist?" Cavan teased.

They returned to the same position, and for a moment when they both pushed inside him again, Christopher had to force himself to ignore the physical sensations in favor of doing what he was meant to do. He looked down into Sebastian's eyes and saw a flash of trepidation there.

-Don't be afraid,- he told him.

Sebastian thought back, *-I have a lot to lose if this goes wrong.-*

-But you have so much to gain when it goes right.- He leaned down and kissed him, then leaned on his elbows, his glove-less hands on either side of Sebastian's head. *-Now just feel your body and let me focus on your mind.-*

He looked inside the jumble that the neural editing had left behind in the dragonel's head, and he could see the damage that had been done. Psychic scars, brutalized pieces of personality and memory, were in desperate need of atten-tion, and there were holes in the fabric of his mind that needed to be filled. Beneath it all, a network of glowing threads, the matrix of the editing process, flickered erratically, trying to repair itself.

First things first. He needed to disable that matrix. It was a tricky prospect, all unwinding and untangling, almost like a form of neurosurgery. Christopher narrowed his focus on the task at hand, forcing the sensations from his body to be just background noise. It was easier said than done with two cocks hammering away at his prostate, but he managed to do it at the cost of his own hard-on. There would be time for such things later.

He found the place in Sebastian's mind where the neural editing had taken root the deepest, and he plucked it out like an errant hair. The dragonel grunted and twitched beneath him, his eyes widening. Connected mind-to-mind as they were, Christopher could feel the pain that lanced through Sebastian, and he regretted it.

-There are moments that might hurt,- he warned the dragonel.

-You don't say. You could have warned me ahead of time.-

-Sorry.-

He returned to his delicate work. Cavan's hands gripped his hips tightly, and he was grateful for the extra contact. It would help him connect.

Christopher spoke in Cavan's mind. *-There are holes in him that need patching. I need you to think about him, everything you know about him and everything the two of you have experienced together.-*

Cavan's mind was fluttering, floating in an ocean of lust, but he responded, *-I'll try.-*

-If you can't, just open yourself to me and let me pull from your memories.-

He could feel the uncertainty in Cavan's emotions as the witch contemplated whether he could trust Christopher or not. To the incubus's relief, he decided to trust him, and all of Cavan's internal shields and protectections melted away.

Christopher entered Cavan's mind and sorted through the memories he found there, searching for the first appearance of the dragonel. When he saw the witch's earliest recollections of childhood, he saw something that startled him so badly he nearly lost his connection with both men.

-*Nicholas!*-

There was a shudder of surprise from Cavan. -*How do you know my brother?*-

Pain shot through Christopher like an arrow at the memory of his dead love's laughter. He blinked away tears and forced himself to look away. Cavan felt the emotion and fell silent, but his thrusts got harder, almost brutal. Christopher's body rocked with it, and he gasped, overcome by the pleasure.

He struggled to regain control and kept looking through Cavan's mind, skimming over the images of Nicholas and searching out the dragonel. He found the memories he was looking for and matched them with the ones that still existed in Sebastian. Where he found no match, he used Cavan's memories to fill in the holes. There were more holes than he would have liked, and it was taking a great deal of time.

-*Hurry,*- Cavan urged. -*I'm going to cum soon.*-

-*Try to hold it off. If you can't, just don't pull out,*- Christopher asked. -*Stay inside me as long as you can.*-

He felt the same thing from Sebastian, as the dragonel, too, was nearing the limit of his endurance. Christopher couldn't have that, and he snapped at Sebastian in his harshest voice.

"Don't you dare cum until I tell you that you can."

The dragonel groaned, but he could feel him controlling his body's responses. His use of his Master voice made Cavan's grip tighten, and he could feel bruises starting to form. The pain made Christopher's neglected cock twitch and start to harden again.

He tried to speed up the process, knowing that this three-way connection wasn't going to last much longer. He filled the gaps, pulled out all of the hooks that the matrix had attached to Sebastian's mind, and removed all of the artificial memories of Azanel that the Countess had tried to implant. Cavan groaned and fell still, trying to hold off his orgasm, and Christopher appreciated the effort. He was nearly finished.

When the last of the damage was healed, he began to withdraw, but on the way out, he saw two tendrils reaching out from Sebastian's solar plexus. One was red and fiery, a pure expression of the ifrit half of his heritage. The other was golden and entirely draconic. The ifrit tendril plunged into Christopher, and the dragon tendril into Cavan. Sebastian spoke to them both at once.

-I recognize you as my Mate. Do you accept this bond?-

Cavan gave his answer aloud, breathless. "Yes."

Christopher's answer was silent. He opened his heart to Sebastian, and the ifrit tendril sank inside. It burrowed down into his own solar plexus, the bright nexus of his life force, where it found an answering demonic bond. The two connected and fused together, joining them in spirit even as their bodies were joining in physical delight. Christopher could feel Sebastian like he was a part of him, and through the dragonel, he could feel Cavan accepting the bond as the Mate to Sebastian's dragon half.

When the two bonds were complete, a glowing flash of energy burst through all of them, and their bodies responded. They came as one, all three of them lost in the ecstasy, physical and otherwise. They fell into a sweaty, sticky pile, overwhelmed and panting.

Sebastian pulled both of them into his arms, kissing them

tenderly. When he pulled away from Christopher, he said, "I didn't wait for permission."

The incubus smiled. "Extraordinary circumstances. I'll forgive you this time."

"Very generous," Cavan commented.

"I'm that way."

Sebastian chuckled. "Liar."

The witch asked, "Did it work?"

Christopher nodded. "Like a charm."

"Hey, bud. I'm the witch. I do the charming around here."

Sebastian laughed. "And yet you're not charming at all. Great mystery of life."

Cavan shook his head, but he was smiling. "You're such an asshole."

"Yeah, but you love me anyway."

"For some unfathomable reason..." Cavan kissed him gently, then pulled away with love shining in his eyes. "It's good to have you back, baby."

"It's good to be back." He turned his golden eyes toward Christopher. "Thank you."

"My pleasure. Literally." The incubus kissed Sebastian. "I look forward to getting to know the real you."

Sebastian put a gentle hand on Christopher's face and the other on Cavan's. "My Mates."

Cavan kissed his palm. "Forever and always. The king is gonna shit himself when he finds out."

The dragonel looked unimpressed. "After everything I've been through, I deserve this."

Christopher agreed. "Yes, you do."

Cavan warned the incubus, "This doesn't mean that I forgive you for everything you've done."

"I wouldn't expect it to."

"As long as we understand each other."

Sebastian stood up and stretched. "I don't know about you guys, but I need a shower. You coming?"

"Probably not room for three," Cavan shrugged.

"One way to find out." Christopher slid off the bed, eager to get cleaned up.

They were pleasantly surprised to find that the shower was large enough for three grown men to shower in simultaneously without tripping over one another too badly. The main shower jet was accompanied by side jets that blasted tingling needles of water, just enough to stimulate the skin but not enough to be irritating or painful. Christopher stood under the big shower head, letting the water rinse down over his head, while Sebastian washed his body. Cavan watched while he cleaned himself up, and when he was done with his military-speed shower, he started washing Sebastian's hair. The dragonel leaned back into him with a smile.

"Christopher, what happened to you?" Cavan asked quietly, his voice barely audible above the water.

It was the first time that the witch had used his name, and he liked the way it sounded on his tongue. "You mean the scars on my back?"

"And the ones on your hands. You really got wracked up."

"Funny you should use the word 'rack,' since that was one of the tools employed," he said. He turned to rinse his back and met Cavan's gaze. "I was brought out of hell as a child, purchased by the Countess for reasons that remain unclear to me. I was less than biddable, you might say, and she had no use for a sub-adult, so I was left with Lord Ashmar and his team to be tamed. This was before he was a lord, back when he was just the guy that ran the local gladiator school."

Sebastian looked surprised. "There are gladiator schools in Numea?"

"Not in Numea. In the Badlands. We're standing in the center of Ashmar's home town."

The dragonel turned to rinse his hair, and Christopher moved out of the way. "That explains a lot."

"Wait," Cavan said, frowning. "So they tortured you?"

"Pretty much from the day I was brought up, yes."

"And hell is an actual place?"

"Yes, it's an actual place."

Sebastian smirked. "Where do you think demons come from, genius?"

Cavan gave him a sour look. "Ass. Hole." He turned back to Christopher. "How old were you?"

"Time is different in hell, but I think I was probably around four, more or less."

He finished rinsing off the soap and stepped out of the shower. Sebastian got rid of the last of his suds, and he and Cavan grabbed towels and followed Christopher into the bedroom. The incubus pulled back the bedspread to cover the sweat and semen stains, then sat down.

Cavan found his clothes and dressed again. While he was hunting for his belt, he asked, "They tortured you right away as soon as you came here, or they waited for you to be older?"

"They waited for me to piss off the Countess. Took less than half an hour, as it happens. The first few sessions were just introductory, mostly beatings. They waited for me to be finished growing before they got too creative."

Sebastian's face was grim. "Those people have a great deal to answer for, and if it kills me, I will make them pay."

"Slow your roll, man," Cavan counseled. "You and what army? The three of us and Kliyo? You're going to need the king to throw in with you, and trust me, he's on Azanel's side."

"That's something I don't understand," Sebastian said. He, too, set about dressing again, putting on his uniform once more. "What is his game? What could he possibly gain from saying that he's my Mate? Anybody could look and see that there's no bond there, especially not now."

Christopher said softly, "The Countess must be in league with him, because all of the memories of you and Azanel on that pier… they're false. They were implanted by the neural editing team."

Cavan frowned. "Why? And how would he ever have come into contact with her?"

"Sometimes we come to Kristal to pick up medicines made in the Kingdom so that our…" He began to say 'live-stock,' but chose to change the word out of deference to his companions. "Our prisoners would have the best care we could give them. Sebastian, the salve that I used for you at the estate was bought here in Kristal, against the laws of Numea."

The witch's frown deepened. "So, what? You want a medal?"

"Cav, hush," Sebastian said. "Do you think it's possible she and Azanel met up in Kristal?"

Christopher hesitated to say more. If he told the rest of what he knew, he would be effectively cutting ties with Numea for good, and his trepidation was making the scar on his hip throb. She knew. Somehow, the Countess knew what he was preparing to do. The pain from the scar was his reminder to watch himself. He took a deep breath and made the only choice that he could make.

"Either in Kristal or at the base north of here."

Both Cavan and Sebastian reacted as if he'd slapped them. "A Numean base?" the dragonel echoed. "Where? We've never heard of any such thing."

Christopher sighed, and the scar on his hip stabbed with pain that made him wince. "Thirty klicks north of here, there's a complete forward operating base for the army. It's under camouflage and would not be visible to your instruments."

"What about our magic?" Cavan challenged. "We used magic to scry for things like that. It's not all tech in the Kingdom."

"I never said it was Numean," Christopher said cautiously.

"Then whose?"

He looked at them, his face reflecting the grimness that he felt.

"Hell's."

CHAPTER NINETEEN

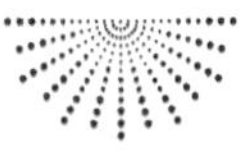

AZANEL

King Goxtli's party, which now included Azanel, returned to the Golden Hall by air, flying in their draconic forms. The flight from Zyros took a little over an hour. The king kept the group to an easy cruising speed, no doubt out of concern for Azanel's injury. The ice dragon appreciated the gesture.

When they reached the Golden Hall, the dragons landed in the courtyard in a wedge formation with King Goxtli at the point. Azanel was at his right hand, a place of honor normally reserved for the heir to the throne. As Sebastian's putative Mate, he occupied that position, nominally until the true heir returned and resumed his proper place. Azanel knew that there were other plans.

The neural editing that the Countess and her unethical scientists had used did more than implant memories of events that had never occurred. It should also have rendered Sebastian meek and ineffectual, an easy target for direction and control. Clearly it had failed on that point. Azanel regretted his deal with the demon now, since she had gained so much more than he had. She had dozens of samples from Sebastian, and all Azanel had was a concussion. It was unfair.

As soon as they landed, the king resumed his humanoid form. The other dragons followed his lead, shifting into their bipedal bodies as well. A group of the king's concubines, males and females of almost every mythric species, surged forward to kneel before him in welcome.

The courtyard was bathed in sunlight, rimmed by hypostyle galleries and marble planters filled with riotously colorful flowers. The marble of the gallery columns and the paving stones beneath their feet was shot through with veins of pure gold that gleamed brightly. The concubines continued the theme of gold, each one dripping with golden baubles and beads, wrapped in a rainbow of silks, each one intricately embroidered with gold thread. The king and all of his kin thought that it was beautiful, but to Azanel, it was gaudy almost beyond endurance. He had had enough gold to last a lifetime.

The senior concubine, the blue dragon who had thought she would become queen upon the death of the king's ifrit Mate, looked around boldly instead of keeping her head bowed. "Sire," she said at last, "where is His Highness?"

Goxtli answered with gravitas and grief. "Not yet fully rescued. He was abducted again before he could be returned."

One of the young males in the harem, a gentle naiad, keened quietly. The sound of his distress made everyone shiver.

"Loris," the king said, walking to the young water nymph. He took the weeping youth into his arms and embraced him. "It is not yet time to mourn. Kliyo and Lt. Waters are in pursuit and will return him. I am sure of it."

Loris clung to his king, his fingers gripping the gold cloth of Goxtli's long jacket. "Is he alive? Is he well?"

"Prince Azanel, come here," the king called.

The ice dragon resented being called like the family dog, but he went to the king's side anyway. "Yes, Your Majesty."

"Is my son well? Can you sense him?"

Truthfully, Azanel had no idea. He closed his eyes and swayed on his feet as if he were reaching out with his mind. He hung his head in a show of defeat.

"They have severed the Mate bond, as we discussed. I cannot tell you anything about him now. I can say that when I saw him last, he was physically in good condition. His mind, though…"

He trailed off, letting the listening concubines draw their own conclusions. Loris wept, and the king continued to hold him.

The blue dragon, whose name escaped Azanel, bowed her head to hide her own tears. "The prince has suffered so much."

"More than you know," Azanel said. He had retrieved his bag, and from it he drew the tablet that held the transcript from Christopher's torture session. "I have the full confession of the Oppressor here."

The king ripped the tablet out of Azanel's hand. "Give me that. I will read this now."

"Your Majesty," the ice dragon began, "I beg you to reconsider. There are things in there that will only bring you pain."

"A father should know what his child was forced to endure," the king responded, his tone stating clearly that he had no intention of being opposed. Azanel backed down, and Goxtli added, "It will help us to know how to help him when he finally comes home."

The king pushed Loris back, but he kissed him on the forehead. "There, there, my pretty. You will stain your face with your tears. Come to me tonight, and I will comfort you."

Loris knelt. "Thank you, Your Majesty."

Goxtli gestured with the tablet to the ice dragon at his

side. "I have this to read, so I will not require your insights. Go to your apartment and rest."

He knew a dismissal when he heard one. He bowed. "Yes, Your Majesty."

The king walked into the palace, his path heading toward the easternmost entry instead of the main doors. He was heading to his Mate's tomb to do his reading, choosing to amplify his own misery. Azanel would never understand the king's propensity for wallowing in his grief.

His own chambers lay in the west wing of the palace, and that is where he went. A healer stepped out of the shadows and into the courtyard, her green robes tastefully trimmed in silver. She was a member of the green dragon tribe, the dragons most able to wield healing magic. He held out his hand to her.

"My lord," she said, curtseying gracefully. "Do you have pain?"

"A residual headache. Nothing more."

"Shall I…"

"I have no need of your services, Catrine."

She nodded. "Yes, sir. I am sorry that…"

He gave her a hard look, and she wisely closed her mouth without finishing the thought. Catrine backed up slowly, leaving him room to pass.

Azanel went up the grand western staircase, built entirely of gold-shot marble, passing golden statutes of dragons coiled around lamp posts, their wings holding up globes that shone with subtle magic to light the way. The illumination was necessary, because the Golden Hall was a cavern that had been dug into the side of a mountain, and there were no windows to be had. He was personally glad for the shadow. Sunlight made his head hurt on the best of days.

At the top of the stairs, his valet met him, standing silently with his hands in the bell sleeves of his otherwise fitted jacket. When Azanel reached him, the human bowed deeply and waited for the prince to pass so he could follow at a respectful distance. Azanel insisted on the deference due someone of his rank, and all of his servants knew it.

He reached the double doors of his apartment, heavy wood painted blue and silver, his house colors. He pushed the doors open and found that his servants had lit incense in preparation for his arrival, and the scent was the first thing to make him truly smile since he had awoken in the healer's tent. He walked through the sitting room and into his bedchamber, and his valet followed, closing and locking the door behind him.

Azanel turned to the man. "Draw a bath and leave me, but be certain to set out my sleeping clothes."

"Yes, Your Highness."

"And send Gort."

The valet bowed. "Yes, Your Highness."

He waited for the man to leave his room, and when he was certain he was alone, he tossed his bag onto the floor and took out his phone. It was a miracle that there was any signal this deep in the cavern, but magic could amplify almost anything. He dialed a pre-programmed number and waited.

After several rings, a female voice purred, "Hello, Azanel."

"Your grandson took my dragonel."

He expected angry denials or a flash or rage, but instead she sounded amused. "I know. Interesting turn of events, wouldn't you say?"

"I thought you could control him."

"I am powerful," the countess said, "but I do have geographical limitations. Christopher is too far away for me to do more than spy on, but I have plans for him when I get closer. Believe me, any soul I own is a soul that I can use any way I please."

"Then you had better use it to make him give Sebastian back," he growled. "This was never part of the plan."

"Not your plan, no."

He felt sick. "You bitch. Have you betrayed me?"

She laughed. "How droll. A traitor who's offended by betrayal. The irony beggars description." Her tone went cold. "Call me a bitch again and I will show you what betrayal really is."

He had known enough demons to know that he was treading a dangerous path. "I'm sorry," he lied. "I'm frustrated by the way things are going."

"You wanted me to plant suggestions and memories. I have done so. Then I facilitated your so-called rescue. What happened from the moment you left Numea was no longer my concern, or in my control."

"I hold you personally responsible for everything that Christopher does."

"And what makes you think that he's not doing everything I want him to do?"

He knew it. She had back-stabbed him. The Oppressor was probably convincing Sebastian to return to GenTel right now, and that would ruin everything. He hung up on her and tossed the phone back into the bag, undressing for his bath with such angry motions that he nearly tore his uniform. The thing was stained anyway, so he spent his fury on the cloth, rending it the way he wished that he could rip the Countess into little bloody pieces.

THE COUNTESS

SHE PUT the phone aside and leaned back in her chair,

crossing her long legs. Her black patent leather stilettos gleamed in the low light. Across the room, a half-minotaur cryptomorph hung whimpering from the x-shaped cross. Lord Ashmar shook out the fatigue in his right arm, the cat o'nine tails dangling from his hand. With his other hand, he wiped perspiration away from his face.

"What is your pleasure, my lady?" her favorite torturer asked.

"I want to watch you beat him to death."

The minotaur moaned, a sound that might have been a wail if he'd been in better shape. She chuckled and pressed a button on her phone, sending a signal to the outside world.

As Ashmar got back to work, the door to the basement chamber opened. A tall woman in leather armor stepped in and walked to the side of the Countess's throne.

"Cassandra," she greeted. "I'm so pleased. Hell's best assassin."

"At your service, my lady," she answered. "Lilith sends her regards."

"And how is my mother these days?"

Cassandra grinned. "The same wretched hag as always."

"The more things change, the more things stay the same." She held out an empty wine glass to the armored woman. "Be a dear, won't you?"

She took the glass and motioned for Ashmar to step back. He obeyed immediately, giving Cassandra a wide berth. She caught the minotaur's blood in the crystal vessel until it was half-filled. She licked some away from the miserable creature's shoulder before she returned to the Countess's side.

"Thank you," she said, accepting the glass. She sipped it. "Ah. So much better when it's fresh, don't you agree?"

Cassandra folded her arms as Ashmar resumed the beating. "What is my first target?"

The Countess thought. Shape-shifting demons had taken

control of all of the cities in Pentepolis, adopting the faces and personae of the rightful leaders. Like her, they were waiting for the time when they could take what should always have been theirs. Their long-distance plan, the one they had been working on so diligently for so many years, was nearly ready to be put into effect.

The cryptomorphs that she had bred were not solely meant to be outlets for the sexual desires of the Community. There were some, of course, who had no other purpose, and others who existed only to be breeders. The vast majority, though, like the disappointment currently expiring on her cross, were bred for one thing: warfare.

In the desert north of Kristal, an army of cryptomorphs trained under the watchful eyes and harsh direction of a cadre of demons from the deepest pits in hell. They were being prepared for the fight of their lives, and she personally could hardly wait to see it start.

It served the Dragon Council right for deciding that demons, though mythrics, were not welcome in the Kingdom. They had cast her and her sisters out, barring them from magic and from feeding upon the nectar that was mythric blood. She had never forgiven them, and now she was close to having her revenge.

Azanel's foolishness had played into her hands. He wanted her help to make the heir to the throne choose him as a Mate, intending to marry into the royal family only to have both the king and the dragonel prince meet unfortunate accidents, leaving only Azanel on the throne. He arranged it so that his fighters arrived a day late to help the King's Claws, leaving the opening for her troops to move in and take the dragonel by force. Once Sebastian was in custody, he asked only for her to do enough psychic damage to make the dragonel compliant and agreeable, and to implant memories that cast Azanel as the wooing lover and potential hero. In return, she would have the dragonel for a year, hers to play with and to express. It wasn't often that she had access to a half-dragon, half-fire elemental to experiment upon. At the end of the year, she made it possible for Azanel to find him again, calling him with the location of Christopher's hidden farm house. The ice dragon had only to "rescue" the dragonel, woo him, and bring him back to the Kingdom to receive all the accolades and presents that a grateful Goxtli would bestow.

Her grandson was supposed to see to the rest. He was meant to be presented to the king as a trophy of war, a slave to be used. The Countess knew that incubi could make anyone desire them, and she knew as well that Goxtli had an addictive personality. Christopher had been carefully trained in how to make a sex partner become addicted to his skills. He had also been trained in other arts, imbued with certain genetic mutations that would make him a key part of her strategy.

She didn't know what he was doing, running away with the dragonel like this. She knew that Christopher had developed soft feelings for his toy, but she couldn't imagine that her grandson would let such ephemeral things as emotions stand in the way of her ambition. It would be in his best interests to see the plan through to fruition.

He was playing his own game, she was sure of it. She just didn't know what that game was.

"Find Christopher and bring him to me," she finally said, answering Cassandra at long last. "When I have talked with him, I want you to take him to King Goxtli as a prisoner."

"And the dragonel?"

"I have what I want from him. Give him to Azanel."

Cassandra bowed. "It will be done, Your Grace."

She bent and kissed the toe of the Countess's shoe, and then she was gone. The Countess turned her attention back to Lord Ashmar's efforts. The half-minotaur's death rattle filled the room, and she raised her glass in a toast to his demise.

Everything was going perfectly to plan.

TO BE CONTINUED....

ABOUT THE AUTHOR

Tiegan Clyne has been writing for longer than most of her friends have been alive. She loves music, dark fantasy, and telling stories. Tiegan is a crazy cat lady in training and an all-around good egg.

She has co-written the successful Reverse Harem Everafter Academy series with Scarlett Snow, and she can be stalked on Facebook:

facebook.com/groups/654717788313017

Have you ever felt like each day you wake up is just another day? Just existing and wondering how to live? Just going through the motions of whatever comes with each new day?

This is the place Diamond once was in this thing called life. We only get one, and it is up to no one else but you to make the best of it! Along the way, God allows people to be either a blessing or a lesson, sometimes both. Not everyone that enters our lives is meant to be there for a lifetime. Most people are there for a season, and it is very imperative to be able to discern when their time in your life expires.

Diamond was at a crossroad in her life and had looked out for those who were near and dear to her heart and just wanted someone to have her back for a change. Her king was not going to fall out of the sky, so it was time for her to get off of her throne so that her king could find his queen.